The fire is hot and the romance sizzles. There are quirky characters, healing of past wounds and a storyline that doesn't slow down. The first in this series set the bar high and I'm looking forward to the next one!

LILY, GOODREADS

Flashpoint hooked me straight in from the start and didn't let go. I enjoyed seeing some familiar characters from Warren's previous series. Packed with non-stop action, danger, and gold nuggets of wisdom and faith, this romantic suspense story will not leave you disappointed.

ALLYSON, GOODREADS

This book was everything that I was hoping for and more. I had an extremely hard time leaving this book behind to go back to real life. I may have taken the book with me everywhere I went for the rest of the day to sneak in a minute of reading here and there. I loved, loved, loved the theme of faith over fear.

MICHAELA, GOODREADS

FLASHPOINT

CHASING FIRE: MONTANA | BOOK 1

A SERIES CREATED BY SUSAN MAY WARREN AND LISA PHILLIPS

SUSAN MAY WARREN

sunrise
PUBLISHING

Flashpoint
Chasing Fire: Montana, Book 1
Copyright © 2024 Susan May Warren
Published by Sunrise Media Group LLC
Print ISBN: 978-1-963372-09-0
Ebook ISBN: 978-1-963372-08-3

This book is a work of fiction. Names, characters, places, and
incidents are either products of the author's imagination or used
fictitiously. Any similarity to actual people, organizations, and/or
events is purely coincidental.

All Scripture quotations, unless otherwise indicated, are taken from
the Holy Bible, New International Version®, NIV®. Copyright
©1973, 1978, 1984, 2011 by Biblica, Inc.™ Used by permission of
Zondervan. All rights reserved worldwide. The "NIV" and "New
International Version" are trademarks registered in the United
States Patent and Trademark Office by Biblica, Inc.™

For more information about Susan May Warren please access the
author's website at susanmaywarren.com.

Published in the United States of America.
Cover Design: Lynnette Bonner

A NOTE FROM SUSIE MAY & LISA

Hey there!

I'm so excited to introduce you to our brand-new novel series! It all started with a simple desire—to solve that timeless problem of what to read next. I wanted to create something that would be your go-to solution, a series that captures the essence of binge-watching your favorite TV series and brings it to the pages of a book—an experience that will captivate and enchant you like never before.

So, I recruited one of my favorite, award-winning, bestselling authors—the talented Lisa Phillips and together, we embarked on a mission to create something truly magical. We've handpicked a team of gifted authors who know how to create poignant characters and riveting stories. Set against the breathtaking backdrop of Montana, specifically in the popular Jude County Firefighters world, the series features both hotshots and smokejumpers who fight a massive wildfire in northern Montana. If you're a fan of the TV series Fire Country, this series is tailor-made just for you!

But here's the best part—our series is so much

more than a collection of standalone novels. It's an ongoing saga, a thrilling narrative that weaves its way through the lives of unforgettable characters, drawing you deeper into their world with every page you turn. Watch out for fan-favorite characters from several Lisa Phillips and Susan May Warren series, new characters you'll fall in love with, and an explosive conclusion.

One of the things that sets our series apart is the emphasis on clean but sizzling romance. Something you could dive into, with the trust of a fantastic story, where danger lurks around every corner, where secrets unravel and hidden truths come to light with each turn of the page. But don't worry, amidst all the heart-pounding action, there'll be moments of respite, joy, and laughter to keep you going.

Our ultimate goal is to create a series that not only entertains but also touches your soul, leaving you with a renewed belief in the incredible power of teamwork, hope, faith and love. And ultimately, the work of Jesus on the cross, as expressed in one of our favorite hymns—It is Well with My Soul—which is a theme that runs through the series.

Every book will release 3 weeks apart—so perfect for your summer reading. Welcome to book 1—and ready to be transported to Ember, Montana—where, love, adventure, and faith intertwine in the most extraordinary ways, making it the perfect summer getaway.

Get ready for a journey you won't soon forget.

Warmly (get it?),

Susan May Warren & Lisa Phillips

When peace like a river attendeth my way,
When sorrows like sea billows roll;
Whatever my lot Thou hast taught me
to say,
"It is well, it is well with my soul!"

CHAPTER 1

Clearly, his last hope at a comeback was about to crash and burn.

Maybe he was being a little melodramatic, but Spenser Storm knew a good story.

Knew how to cater to an audience, knew when a script was a disaster.

And this one had flames all over it.

Yes, the screenplay had all the right ingredients — a winning western retelling of a widow and her son who leaned on the help of two strangers to save her land. And they were shooting on location in Montana at a real abandoned western town rebuilt and redressed for the movie, complete with a jail and a church.

They'd even hired an up-and-coming country music star to write original music.

The problem was, the producer, Lincoln Cash, picked the wrong man to die.

Not that Spenser Storm had a say in it — he'd been given all of sixteen lines in the one-hundred-twenty-page script. But he wanted to ask, while waving flags and holding a megaphone — *Who killed off the hero at the*

1

end of a movie? Had no one paid any attention to the audience during the screening of *Sommersby*?

He didn't care how many academy-acclaimed actors were attached to this movie. Because everyone—even he—would hate the fact that their favorite action hero ended up fading into eternity. And he wasn't talking about himself, but the invincible Winchester Marshall.

Perfect. Spenser should probably quit now and go back to herding cattle.

"Back to ones!" Indigo, the first Assistant Director, with her long black hair tied back, earphones around her neck, raised her hand.

Spenser nudged his mare, Goldie, back to the position right outside town. Sweat trickled down his spine, and he leaned low so a makeup assistant could wipe his brow.

Yeah, something in his gut said trouble. It didn't help that all of Montana had become a broiler, even this early in the summer—the grass yellow, the temperature index soaring, turning even the wind from the pine-saturated mountains into the breath of hades.

But saving the movie wasn't Spenser's job. No, his job was to sit pretty atop his horse and smile for the camera, those gray-blue eyes smoldery, his body tanned and a little dusty, his golden-brown hair perfectly curled out of his black Stetson, his body buff and muscled under his blue cotton shirt and a leather vest.

He wore jeans, black boots, and could have walked off the set of *Yellowstone*. No, *swaggered* off the set. Because he wasn't a fool.

They'd cast him as eye candy. With sixteen lines

and the guy who got the girl at the end. Spenser was the sizzle for the audience who was too young for Winchester Marshall, the lead of the movie, although Spenser was just a couple years younger.

But, like Lincoln Cash said when he signed him, Spenser had a special kind of appeal.

The kind that packed the convention floor at comic cons around the world.

Wow, he hated comic cons. And adults who dressed up as Iwonians and spoke a language only created in fanfic world. If he never heard the name Quillen Cleveland again, he'd die a happy man.

He hated to mention to Lincoln that the fans who loved *Trek of the Osprey* might not enjoy a western called *The Drifters*, but a guy with no screen credits to his name for five years should probably keep his mouth shut when accepting a role.

At least according to his agent, Greg Alexander.

Keep his mouth shut, deliver his lines, and maybe, hopefully, he'd be back in the game.

"We need a little more business from the extras." Director Cosmos Ferguson wore a *Drifters* T-shirt, jeans and boots, and his own cowboy hat. "Feel free to cause more havoc on the set."

Behind him, Swen, from SFX stepped out of the house, checking on the fire cannons for the next shot. The set crew had trailered in an old cabin for today's shoot—a real structure with a porch and a stone chimney that rose from the tattered wooden roof—and plunked it down in a valley just two hundred yards from the town, with a corral for the locally sourced horses. It was a postcard of bygone days.

Was it only Spenser, or did anyone else think it

3

might be a bad idea to light a fire inside a rickety wooden house that looked already primed for tinder?

"Quiet on the set!"

Around him, the world stopped. The gaffers, the grips, the second team, the stuntmen, even, it seemed, the ripple of wind through the dusty one-horse ghost town-slash-movie set.

Not even Goldie moved.

"Picture's up!" Indigo said.

At least Spenser could enjoy the view. The sky stretched forever on both sides of the horizon, the glorious Kootenai mountains rising jagged and bold to the north, purple and green wildflowers cascading down the foothills into the grasslands of the valley.

"Roll sound!"

A hint of summer night hung in the air. Perhaps he'd grab a burger at the Hotline Bar and Grill in Ember, just down the street from Motel Bates, where the cast was staying. Okay, the lodging wasn't that bad, but—

"Action."

The extras, aka cowboys, burst to life, shooting prop guns into the air just before Winchester Marshall, aka Deacon Cooper, rode in, chasing them away with his own six-shooter. They raced out of town, then Deacon got off his horse, dropped the reins, and checked the pulse of the fallen extra. "Hawk, C'mere. I think this is one of the cowboys from the Irish spread."

Spenser's cue to ride on screen, dismount and confirm, then stand up and stare into the horizon, as if searching for bad guys.

Seemed like a great way for a guy to get shot. But again, he wasn't in charge of the script.

4

So, he galloped onto the set, swung his leg over Goldie's head, jumped out of the saddle, and sauntered up. He gave the scene a once over, met Winchester-slash-Deacon's eyes with a grim look, and nodded. Then he turned and looked at the horizon, his hands on his hips, while the camera zoomed in, trouble in his expression.

"Cut!" Cosmos said as he walked over to them. "I love the interaction between you two." He turned away, motioning to Swen.

What interaction? Spenser wanted to ask, but Winchester—"Win" to the crew—rose and clamped a hand on Spenser's shoulder. "One would think you grew up on a horse the way you rode up."

"I did," Spenser said, but Win had already turned away, headed to craft services, probably for a cold soda.

"Moving on. Scene seventeen," Indigo said. "Let's get ready for the house fire."

Spenser jogged over to Goldie and grabbed her reins, but a male stunt assistant came up and took hold of the mare's halter. "I've got her, sir."

Spenser let the animal go and headed over to the craft table set up under a tented area, back from the set, near the two long connected trailers brought in for the actors. The Kalispell Sound and Light truck was parked next to an array of rental cars, along with the massive Production trailer, where the wardrobe department kept their set supplies, including a locked container for the weapons.

"That was a great scene." This from the caterer, a woman named Juliet, whose family owned the Hot Cakes Bakery in Ember. She wore her brown hair back in a singular braid and handed him a sandwich, nodding to drinks in a cooler. Not a fancy setup, but this far out in the sticks, they were beggars. Cosmos had also ordered a hot breakfast from the Ember Hotline every morning.

"Thanks." Spenser unwrapped the plastic on his sandwich. "This bread looks homemade."

"It is. The smoked chicken is from the Hotline, though." She winked, but it wasn't flirty, and continued to set out snacks—cookies and donuts.

The sandwich reminded him a little of the kind of food that Kermit, the cook for the Flying S Ranch, served during roundup, eaten with a cold soda, and a crispy pickle.

Sheesh, what was he doing here, back on a movie set? He should be home, on his family's ranch...

Or not. Frankly, he didn't know where he belonged.

He turned, eating the sandwich, and watched as lead actress Kathryn Canary, seated on a high director's chair, dressed in a long grimy prairie dress, her blonde hair mussed, ignored a makeup assistant applying blood to her face and hands. She held her script in one hand, rehearsing her lines as Blossom Winthrop, the heroine with Trace Wilder, playing the role of her husband, Shane Winthrop.

Who was about to die.

He hadn't seen Trace since his last movie, but the man seemed not to remember their short stint on *Say You Love Me*.

Spenser would like to forget it too, frankly. Another reason why he'd run back to the family ranch in central Montana.

It all felt surreal, a marriage of Spenser's worlds— the set, busy with gaffers setting up lighting, and the sound department fixing boom mics near the house, the set dresser putting together the scene. And then, nearby, saddles lined up along the rail of a corral where horses on loan from a nearby ranch nickered, restless with the heat.

Cowboys, aka extras, sat in holding with their hats pushed back, drinking coffee, wearing chaps and boots. All they were missing were the cattle grazing in the distance. Maybe the smell of burgers sizzling on Kermit's flat grill.

Bandit, the ranch dog, begging for scraps.

They did, however, have a cat, and out of the corner of his eye, Spenser spotted Bucky Turnquist, age eight, who played Dusty Winthrop, chase the tabby around the set. His mother, Gemma, had already hinted that, as a single mom, she might be interested in getting to know Spenser better.

Now, she talked with one of the villain cowboys, laughing as he got on his horse.

"You guys about ready?" Cosmos had come back from where the cameramen were setting up, the grip team working to shade the light for the shot, on his way to Kathryn and Trace, who were rising from their chairs.

One of the SFX guys raised a hand from where they set up the cannons that would 'fire' the house. Not a real fire, not with the burn index so high in this part of crispy, dry Montana. But enough that it would generate heat and look real.

And enough that they'd asked the local wildland fire team on set to keep an eye on anything that might get out of hand. He'd caught sight of the handful of firefighters dressed in their canvas pants, steel-toed boots, yellow Nomex shirts, and Pulaskis hanging out

7

near the fire. They'd brought up a fire truck, too, with a hose ready to deploy water.

"Get a hose over here, Emily!" A man wearing a vest, the word Command on the back, directed a woman, her blonde hair in a tight ponytail, to pull up a hose nearer the building, and hand it over to another firefighter. Then she ran back to the truck, ready to deploy.

According to the script, the cowboys would fire at the house, and then a stuntman would run out, on fire, and collapse to the ground. Cue Kathryn, as Blossom, to run in with a shirt she'd pulled from the hanging laundry to snuff it out while the cowboys attempted to kidnap her.

She'd panic then, and scream for Dusty, and only then would the kid run from the barn. They'd be surrounded, swept up by the villains and taken away while poor Shane died.

At which point the guy would go down to the Hotline for a nice cool craft beer and a burger, then tomorrow, catch a ride to Kalispell and head back to his air-conditioned apartment in LA.

"Ready on Special Effects?" Indigo shouted. She'd reminded him that this wasn't *Trek of The Osprey* and that he wasn't the star here when he'd headed to the wrong trailer on day one.

Whatever. Easy mistake.

"Ready!" This from Swen, who stood away from the house. The cowboys were already in place and Blossom stood at the clothesline in the yard, away from the house.

"Quiet on set!" Indigo shouted. She glanced at Cosmos, who nodded. "Roll Camera. Roll Sound."

A beat. "Action!"

And that's when he spotted little Bucky, still chasing the cat, scooting under the house on his hands and knees.

At the front of the house, a window burst and flames licked out of it.

"Wait!"

The next window burst. More fire.

"Bucky's in there!" Where was his mother? It didn't matter. He took off for the back of the house.

The cowboys in the front yard whooped, shots fired, and of course, the stuntman stumbled out in his firesuit and flopped onto the front yard.

Blossom screamed and ran to put out the fire just as Spenser reached the back of the house.

The fire seemed real enough, with the roof now catching. "Bucky?"

With everyone's gaze on the action, no one had seen him wriggle under the porch. Spenser hit his knees. "Bucky?"

There. Under the middle of the house, curled into a ball, his hands over his ears. "Bucky, C'mere!"

He was crying now, and Spenser saw why—the entire front porch had caught fire.

Sparks dropped around him. The grass sizzled.

Aw—Spenser dropped to his belly and army crawled into the center of the house, coughing, his eyes watering. He grabbed Bucky's foot, yanked.

Bucky kicked at him, split his lip. Blood spurted.

"C'mon kid!"

He grabbed Bucky's arms and jerked him close, wrapping him up, holding him. "It's okay. C'mon, let's get out of here." Smoke billowed in from where the porch fell, a line of fire blocking their escape. But out the back—

Then, suddenly, a terrible crack rent the building, and with a thunderous crash, the old chimney tumbled down. Dust and rock crashed through the cabin, tore out the flooring, and obliterated the porch.

Blocked their exit.

Spenser grabbed Bucky and pulled him close, holding his breath, then expelling the dust, his body wracking with coughs. And Bucky in his arms, screaming.

When he opened his eyes, fire burned around them, a cauldron of very real, very lethal flames.

"Stop! Stop the film! There's someone inside there!"

Or at least Emily thought so. She still wasn't quite sure if that was a person or an animal she'd seen dive under the burning house.

In truth, she'd been stationed by her fire truck, watching the house burn, trying not to let her gaze drift back to the beautiful and amazing Spenser Storm, standing near craft services.

The Spenser Storm.

From *Trek of the Osprey*. Quillen Cleveland in the flesh, all grown up and ruggedly handsome, dressed in western getup: leather vest, chaps, black boots, and a Stetson over his burnished golden-brown hair, those gray-blue eyes that a girl could get lost in. He even wore that rakish, heart-thumping smile. The man who saved the galaxy, one world at a time, there he was...

Eating a sandwich.

She'd spotted him almost right off this morning when she'd arrived with fellow hotshot Houston James and her fire boss, Conner Young. The Special

Effects department had called in the local Jude County Hotshots as a precaution.

Not a terrible idea given the current fire index.

The SFX supervisor, Swen, had briefed the hotshots before the event—squibs of dust on a lead that would explode to imitate bullets hitting the building. They'd walked through the system that would create the explosion, a tank filled with propane, rigged to burst the window and release a fireball.

She'd expected the bomb, but when the squibs detonated, Emily nearly hit the dirt.

Nearly. But *didn't*. So, take that, panic attack. No more PTSD for her, thank you ten years of therapy.

Except, the explosion hadn't gone quite like they'd hoped. Sure, the gas dissipated into the air, but somehow cinder had fallen onto the porch.

The entire old wooden porch burst into flames.

Black smoke cluttered the sky, and if she were a spotter, via a fire tower or a plane, she'd be calling in sparks to the local Ember fire department. Which would then deploy either the Jude County Hotshots or, if the fire started further in, the Jude County Smokejumpers. The first and last line of defense against fire in this northwest corner of Montana.

About as far away as she could get from her failures, thank you.

Not anymore. This was a new season, a new start, and this time...*this time* the shrapnel of the past wasn't going to eviscerate her future.

So, she'd stood by the truck, waiting for the signal from Conner. Tall, brown hair, calm, he'd been brought in to command the team for the summer while Jed Ransom, their former boss, now crewed the Missoula team.

And that's when, in her periphery, she'd spotted—
was that a *person* diving under the back of the house?
Black boots disappeared under the footing of the
cabin.

Were they out of their *mind?*

Maybe it was an animal—cats sometimes ran
toward a fire instead of away.

"Boss!" —She had nearly shouted, but that would
carry, and with the house on fire, the director only
had one take. Instead, she'd headed to the house—

The chimney simply collapsed. A crack, then
thunder as the entire handmade stone chimney
crumbled. She dropped to her knees, her hands over
her head, as dust, rock, and debris exploded out from
the house.

From the front came shouts and shooting, the
cameras still rolling. She lifted her head, blinking as
the dust settled. The inferno now engulfed the front of
the house, moving fast toward the back, the roof half-
collapsed. "Boss!"

And then a thought clicked in—*black boots.* "It's
Spenser! Spenser Storm is under the building!"

No one heard her over the roar of the fire, the
shouts from the street.

No one died today. Not on her watch.

C'mon, Emily, think!

She ran over to the truck, grabbed her Pulaski, and
then opened the cab door and hit the siren. It screamed
over the set as she scrambled toward the house.

Flames kicked out the side windows now, the heat
burning her face. She pulled up her handkerchief and
dug at the rubble.

The siren kept whining, sweat burning down her

back, but in a second, she'd created a hole. She dropped to her knees. "Hello? Hello?"

"In here!"

Smoke cluttered the area, but she made out—yes, Spenser Storm, and a kid.

Oh no, the little Turnquist kid, the son of one of the locals in town.

Emily's eyes watered, but she crawled inside the space, pushing the Pulaski out in front of her. "Grab hold!"

Hands gripped her ankles. "Emily! Get out of there!"

Conner's voice.

"Grab the ax!" she shouted.

Spenser's hand gripped the ax, his other around the kid.

"Pull me out!" this, to Conner.

It was everything she could do to hold onto the Pulaski as they dragged them out from the crawl space. She cleared the building, then launched to her feet even as Conner tried to push her away.

Spenser Storm appeared, like a hero crawling from the depths of hell. The child clung to him, his face blackened, his wardrobe filthy and sooty, his eyes reddened, coughing as he kicked himself free.

"Bucky!" His mother ran toward him, but someone grabbed her back.

Instead, superstar Winchester Marshall, aka Jack Powers, aka whatever hunk he was playing in this western, was right there, pulling the kid from Spenser's arms.

Cosmos pushed through to grab Spenser, helped him to his feet. Spenser bent over, coughing.

"Water! Make a hole!" Cosmos yelled, leading Spenser away.

The movie star didn't even look at Emily as he stumbled to safety.

"C'mon—we need to put out this fire." Conner took off for the hose.

She ran to the truck, still coughing, turned off the siren, then, seeing Houston's signal, she hit the water.

The hose filled, and in a moment, water doused the house, spray saturating the air.

She leaned over, caught her knees, breathing hard. Watched as the fire died. Listened to the roaring on set, and in her heart, subside.

Felt the knot unravel.

No, no one died today. Especially not Spenser Storm.

She stood up, still hauling in breaths. She'd *saved* Spenser Storm. Holy Cannoli.

No, no she wouldn't make a fool of herself and ask for an autograph. And certainly not tell him, ever, that she'd had at least two *Tiger Beat* centerfold posters of him in his Osprey uniform—a pair of black pants, boots and white shirt, leather vest, holding a Vortex Hand Cannon. Never mind mentioning that she'd once attended a Comic-Con just to stand in line for a photo op. He wouldn't remember her, right? Or her status as a Stormie—a member of his official fan club?

"Hey!"

She looked up. Froze.

Spenser Storm was headed her direction, holding a water bottle, his eyes watering, looking like he'd just, well, been pulled from a fire. "You okay?"

She nodded, her eyes widening. C'mon words—

"I just wanted to say thanks." He held out his hand. "You saved my life back there. And Bucky's."

She nodded again. *C'mon words!*

"Maybe I can buy you a drink down at the Hotline sometime?"

"Mmmhmm." *That didn't count!*

Then he smiled, a thousand watts of pure charisma, sunshine and star power, winked, and walked away.

And right then, right there, she nearly died.

CHAPTER 2

"THERE SHE IS. OUR HERO."

Emily walked out of the locker room area into the lounge of the Jude County Hotshots HQ—a space with sofas, a television, a small kitchen with a long table, currently filled with boxes from Backdraft Pizza.

She raised a hand to fellow hotshot Houston James, who sat, also freshly showered, with his guitar and a piece of pepperoni pizza on a napkin on the coffee table. He was plunking out a song, humming. He knew fire, wore a few scars up his neck, his burns leaving him bald. But he never talked about the scars and seemed to have put it behind him.

"Not a hero. Just doing my job."

"I dunno. I heard you're Storm's new personal bodyguard." Orion Price, barely twenty-two, had his feet up on the coffee table, finishing off a box of wings. "I hear he'd be toast without you."

"Not even a little." Although her body still hummed, despite her attempts to shrug away his wink. Sheesh. It wasn't like she would see him again.

Note to self...avoid the Hotline. She should thank

her personal panic button for not saying something stupid to him. "Listen. Storm can take care of himself. He did all his own stunts on *Trek of the Osprey*."

Silence.

Oh, shoot.

"Really." Orion grinned.

"So, I read. Whatever."

"I knew his name sounded familiar." This from Charlie Benning, a new recruit despite being in his early forties and a long-time firefighter. Charlie stood at the sink, doing dishes. Nice guy, salt-and-pepper hair, a thin layer of matching whiskers. He was quiet, easygoing, and capable.

Apparently, he came from some rescue squad team out of state. Somewhere called Last Chance County.

"It's just the longest running sci-fi family drama in history." Emily grabbed a napkin and perused the pizza choices.

"I loved that show when I was a kid. Quillen was such a hottie," said Joanna, aka JoJo Butcher, her roommate and a smokejumper with the crew. She and the team had spent the day inspecting and refolding their chutes after airing them out in the hanging room. She helped herself to pizza and sat on the sofa next to Dakota Masterson, another newbie, although nearly thirty, who'd joined the crew just this season.

In fact, they had more newbies than regulars here. Charlie and Dakota and a woman known just as Sanchez, as well as four tight-knit, quiet guys who'd transferred from a different team—Hammer, Saxon, Kane, and Mack. Tough guys, they exuded a military aura, except for Mack, who seemed like someone's kid brother.

They kept their mouths shut and did the work,

and that's what counted. And, in fact, at the moment were in the attached gym, lifting, a little classic rock — *Born to be Wild* by Steppenwolf — playing over their grunting.

The only other seasoned firefighters were their crew boss, Conner, and Orion Price, a second-year veteran from Ember — the other former members having joined the smokejumpers crew.

"I suppose." Emily purposely kept her voice cool after JoJo's statement. No one needed to know about her obsession. "If you like space-cowboy adventure television."

Oh, she was only making it worse, given JoJo's smile. What. *Ever.* She scooped up a lonely piece of cheese pizza and sat on the faded tweed couch next to Dakota. "Hey."

He nodded, his gaze on the television where he was currently murdering someone in some video game.

"You're pretty good with that gun," she said.

He lifted a shoulder. "Lots of practice time." Although, even as he said it, his character died.

"Sorry."

"Not your fault." He set the controller on the table. "So, yeah, how'd you know Storm was under the house?"

"I saw him go in. Or at least I saw his boots. Or I thought I did — okay, let's say it was a gut call." She took a bite of pizza. Cold, and the crust had turned to rubber. Ew.

"A call you nearly died because of." Charlie turned from the sink, his hands in a towel.

"Not surprised," said Conner who'd come from his

nearby office to stand in his doorway, one shoulder against the frame. "Her parents are—"

"Stop, please, Un—Um, Chief."

Conner raised an eyebrow.

But frankly, it had taken her years to climb out from under her parents' shadow, and even now, to not let the past cripple her.

Today had been a victory in more than just one way. Sure, she'd met Spenser Storm, but more importantly, *bam!*—PTSD, was going down, one call out at a time.

"Who are her parents?" Houston asked.

"Her mom's with the NSA, and her dad's an Army Ranger. They run a SAR team," Dakota said.

She stared at Dakota. "Really?"

He shrugged. "My sister-in-law is on the team. A K-9 specialist." He picked up the controller again. "All I hear about at family events is the amazing Jim Micah and his super-smart wife Lacey who now run an international SAR team with the Red Cross."

Now Emily was the one to raise an eyebrow. Issues, anyone?

But Miles Dafoe chose that moment to walk into the room. "Micah, Young, in my office." He gestured down the hall and Emily got up, leaving the pizza behind.

When they reached his office, he gestured to the chairs.

Behind his desk, the massive picture window looked out upon the tarmac where the smokejumper planes sat, waiting. Beyond that was the training facility for the teams, including the jump platforms, and the burn lines they'd dug.

She'd passed without a hiccup, and today had been a sort of personal final test.

Hooah.

Commander Dafoe leaned against the front of his desk, his arms folded. "So many things in my head about today. Not sure where to start." He reminded her in a way of Gil Grissom from CSI—stern, capable, thoughtful. He wore his dark hair short, salt at the temples, his shirt sleeves folded up, a pair of canvas trousers.

"How about, good save, Emily?" Conner took a sip of his coffee.

Miles considered him. Finally, "I don't know whether to put you on probation or give you a promotion. But it was reckless, Em. You know that, right?"

She swallowed, her throat drying. Nodded.

"I'm just glad your team was there to pull you out. But what possessed you to climb under a burning porch—"

She opened her mouth, and he held up a hand.

"Besides Spenser Storm."

Oh. "Just wanted to save lives, Commander."

"It's in her blood." Conner took another sip of coffee.

Oh please. "Listen, I just want to prove that I can be a contributing member of the team. I don't need any favors because of my dad." She gave Uncle Conner a pointed look. "I earned my spot here."

A beat. And thankfully no one brought up the incident in Benson, or even that moment the first week of training when an explosion ignited the field. She'd hit the dirt, hands over her ears. Could she help it that her earliest memory was exactly that—an explosion that had nearly gotten her killed? But she got back up. Kept going.

Finished training.

And today, saved two lives. "How's Bucky?"

"He's good. A little shaken."

"More than a little, I'll guess," she said and wanted to clamp her hand over her mouth. Whoops. But, "At least he's safe. Maybe he can talk to a trauma counselor or something."

Miles nodded.

"If we had one in the area," Conner said.

"With all these hotshots and emergency personnel around, not one trauma counselor?"

"We're too busy keeping the trauma from happening," Miles said. "Which brings me to today. That fire could have started a major conflagration."

"It's so dry out," Conner said. "We haven't had a summer like this for years—back when Jed took over the team."

"Yeah. Same conditions going into this summer. Low snowfall this season, early spring, no rain—the entire Kootenai forest is a tinderbox, and one lightning strike, one out-of-control campfire—"

"One special effect explosion—" Conner interjected.

Miles pointed at him. "Right. It could all go up and get out of control quickly."

"They were smart to call in the team," Emily said.

Miles nodded. Smiled. Looked at her.

"What?"

"I just got off the phone with Lincoln Cash, the producer of *The Drifters*, thanking our team for being there. And suggested to him that probably, they need someone there from our team to keep an eye on their special effects, bring in a team when needed, be on site to divert any possible problems."

"Sounds like a good...wait." Emily swallowed. "Wait, wait—"

"Emily, you know they already trust you. And the likelihood of anything happening again is small, but possible, so..."

"Is this—?" She turned to Conner. "Are you trying to protect me? Is this my dad, calling you about..." She clamped her mouth shut. Drew in a breath.

Conner met her gaze.

"About what?" Miles asked.

She stared at Conner, her heart in her throat. He just kept her gaze and said, "Nothing."

Silence, then, "This is about protecting our forest, and the people on the set, and you showed not only bravery, but quick thinking with setting off the siren. If you hadn't been there, it's possible there would have been casualties."

Oh. She turned, looked at Miles. "So, what am I supposed to do?"

"Be on set, every day. Consult with the SFX team. Call in reinforcements if needed. Be ready for trouble. And overall, keep everyone safe. Or at least away from fire."

She glanced again at Conner. "So I'm off the team?"

"Not off. Just...diverted."

Her mouth tightened. Oh, she knew what this was.

This was her father, stepping in to keep her safe, again. Seriously, she couldn't outrun the man.

"Fine."

"Good. I'll tell Cash that you'll be on set in the morning."

Perfect. Just spectacular. Best summer of her life.

"Good thing luck was on your side, kid. What were you *thinking*?" Cosmos's shout could probably be heard outside Spenser's tiny trailer where Spenser sat under the bright lights as Lincoln, Cosmos, and Swen Oliver, the SFX guy, tried to untangle the disaster on set.

"I was thinking there was a kid who was going die," Spenser said, less loudly. No need to have the entire cast assemble outside the door. Maybe get the conversation on social media. "I was thinking, where was his mother? And why did we cast a kid with no acting background? He's running around the set chasing a cat—he should be in school. Back when I was growing up, we were required to be in school three hours a day."

"It's summer," Lincoln said. "He's out of school, but I agree, we need a designated guardian for the kid, someone who understands how dangerous a movie set can be."

"How about his mother?" Cosmos said.

"Parents are the last people you want on set. If they're not flirting with the actors, they're pestering the assistants," Spenser said. "And the kid is the last thing they think about."

Lincoln raised an eyebrow. "Spoken like a child with a parent on set."

"Grandparent. At least after my dad passed."

"He's still missed," Cosmos said. "Nobody did stunts like Hank Storm."

"Except his crazy superstar son who we clearly overpaid for this movie if he's going to die on us," Lincoln said.

"I agree I'm overpaid—especially since I only have sixteen lines! Sheesh, with the amount of screen time I get, maybe I should be the kid's guardian."

Silence.

"I was kidding."

Lincoln looked at Cosmos, raised an eyebrow.

"Really. Kidding. Guys—"

"I like it. You know what it feels like to be a kid on set," Cosmos said. "And we only have two more weeks of shooting left."

"That's not the only thing," Lincoln said. "I talked with Miles Dafoe, down at the Jude County Hotshot HQ. He thinks we need someone from the team here full time for the rest of shooting to make sure we don't have any more accidents like today."

Swen had stood by the door all this time. Tall, swarthy, blond, he came from LA in his own trailer full of effects, his own staff who moved around the set outside the movie crew. "I have my own safety crew. I don't need help."

"Where were they today?" Spenser said. "Because the only one with a hose was that hotshot team."

Swen's eyes narrowed, then he took a breath. "And now a *model* is telling me how to run my business."

Spenser's mouth opened. *What—?*

"Okay, that's enough," Lincoln said. "Swen, we trust you, but this can't happen again, okay? I now have to have a chat with the insurance people to assure them that this was a fluke. But if I have to have a firefighter on set to keep them calm, I will."

And just like that, Spenser's mind fixed on the woman.

The woman who'd saved his life. Granted, he'd been heading for the exit, but without her clearing a path, and maybe helping him out before the entire house fell in...

Really pretty, blonde hair, blue eyes, curvy, even in her uniform. In truth, he'd noticed her *before* the catastrophe.

He had mentioned buying her a drink at the Hotline. Sort of sounded lame against her heroics, now that he thought about it.

Besides she'd probably shrugged it off by now. Just another day at work.

"Swen," Cosmos said, "make sure she has a rundown of all the special effects in the script."

Swen's jaw tightened, but he nodded. "I'm going to talk to my crew, see what went wrong." He pushed open the door.

Outside, the night was falling, with twilight across the mountains to the east, settling purple into the valley. Spenser's stomach growled.

Lincoln reached out to shut the door.

Looked at Spenser.

"What?"

Cosmos, too, hadn't moved.

"We're just wondering if this is somehow a repeat of what happened on *Say You Love Me*."

He blinked at them. "Seriously? That was five years ago. *Five*."

"Jayla Pierce is out of jail," Cosmos said. "Did you know that?"

He stilled. Swallowed. "No."

"I would have thought Greg had called you."

Him too. "There's a permanent restraining order against her."

"You think that's going to stop someone who snuck into your trailer, waited for you, and then trapped you inside, demanding that you marry her?" He finger quoted the last words.

Marry was such a vague word for what went down.

"Part of her plea deal was that she can't even be in the same state."

"I'm just saying, be on the lookout." Cosmos rose. "Frankly, Spenser, I hope all the hype is worth it."

"Sixteen lines. I promise they'll be Academy worthy." He held up three fingers.

"We can't have what happened in *Say You Love Me* happen here, okay?"

Meaning his complete and utter shut down? His inability to finish the movie, thanks to the trauma?

"We're good. I'm good. It's all good."

Lincoln hid a smile.

"Good." Cosmos pointed at him. "Get some sleep. You're delivering six of those lines tomorrow, during the rescue scene." He saluted Lincoln. "I saw some of the rushes from today—despite the fire, we got a lot of good film."

He walked out the door, letting it bang behind him.

Two down, one to go. Spenser looked at Lincoln. "Really, Jayla is not coming back."

"How about that crazy guy from comic con?"

"The one who wanted me to read his script? No. He's harmless."

"What about that podcaster you punched—"

"He made a lewd comment about my modeling. And while I would sort of like to forget I did that, I don't need anyone reminding me of how horrible that year was with comments that…well, weren't exactly PG. You would have punched him too, Linc."

Lincoln smiled. "Maybe. But I took a big chance on you, Spenser. And not just because of my relationship with Greg, but also because I had a stalker once. So I know what it feels like to need a fresh start. And, I know how getting back into the groove can be a little overwhelming. Three years roping cattle can just about flush the acting blood out of your veins, even from a legacy like you, so that's why you have so few lines. You do well here, and I have other scripts I'm looking at, okay?"

"Appreciate that, Linc." He got up, met Lincoln's grip. "I promise, I'm ready. I won't let you down."

Linc didn't let go of his hand. "I know it's been a bit of a road back since Chanel died. Your great grandmother left massive shoes to fill. Add to that the breaking out of the stigma of being a child actor, and I know this movie is a big risk for you. You got this."

Shoot. Until this moment, he'd actually felt that indeed, he had this.

And then Lincoln looked him in the eye with so much faith. As if he actually believed him. "And I didn't overpay. Just for the record. You and your million-dollar smile are going to fill the theaters."

Right. He didn't know why, with that comment, he wanted to get up and walk out the door, straight back to the Flying S Ranch. Forget this crazy charade.

Return to the only life that had made him feel whole.

Until, of course, it didn't.

Maybe he didn't know where he belonged.

Lincoln pushed out the door, then held it for Spenser. "You need a ride back to Ember?"

"Naw. I brought my bike."

"Bike?"

"Vintage Victory, 1200 Octane."

"Now that's a bike." Lincoln let the door to the trailer close behind him.

The sun was just dipping beyond the craggy mountains to the west, the smell of summer in the air.

"I think Cosmos and I are grabbing a pizza with Winchester Marshall, if you want to join us." Lincoln headed to his rental car.

Spenser walked over to his bike, black with chrome wheels, and grabbed his helmet. "Naw. I think I'm going to go to the Hotline, grab a burger."

Lincoln lifted a hand, and Spenser climbed onto his bike.

"Maybe I can buy you a drink down at the Hotline sometime?"

So maybe not totally lame. And, like Cosmos said, maybe luck was on his side.

CHAPTER 3

EMILY WASN'T HERE FOR *HIM*.

That was crazy, right? To sit at the counter of the Hotline for—she checked her watch—thirty-two minutes waiting for a certain movie star to walk in like, what…he came to see her?

Actually meant what he'd said about buying her a beer?

She didn't even *drink* beer.

Yeah, this was stupid. She should just make the order of a burger and waffle fries to go and walk home the three blocks to the house she shared with JoJo Butcher and Sanchez.

Then she might not look quite so pitiful sitting by herself in a restaurant filled with hotshots, smokejumpers, and various other locals. The Trouble Boys, as she decided to dub them—Hammer, Saxon, Kane, and Mack—played pool in the adjoining room, and some of the smokejumpers were shooting darts in the back. She knew just a few besides JoJo—Logan, the team lead, and Booth, a long-haired, bearded, dark and mysterious sort who mostly sat on a stool and watched the group. Then there was Nova Burns, gorgeous, with her long red hair who was laughing and talking trash with her team. But that's what happened when you were a legacy firefighter. Apparently, her uncle, Jock, had been a legendary team leader before he was killed.

Even Tirzah Hart, their pilot, was sitting at the bar, talking with Booth.

And then there was Emily. Sitting alone. On a stool. Watching a rerun of the Stanley Cup playoffs on the flatscreen.

Waiting for a movie star to show up and buy her a drink.

She wanted to bang her head on the counter.

She motioned to the barkeep, a woman with black hair, gauged ears, tattoos down her arm. One of them was the name of her deceased brother, Bo, a smokejumper who'd died years ago in a fire. "Hey, Patrice, go ahead and make that order to go, okay?"

"Another root beer?" Patrice pointed to her glass.

"Sure." She pushed it away, sighed.

"You okay?" Patrice picked up the glass, wiped the circle of moisture on the bar.

"Probably. Definitely." She watched the goalie on the screen capture the puck in his pocket. Recognized the team—the Minnesota Blue Ox. Her dad knew a guy who played for them, or maybe had played for them. Something. He was a fan, at any rate.

She half-expected him to text her.

"Good." Patrice went to fill up her drink while Emily glanced over her shoulder at the smokejumpers. JoJo was laughing, completely comfortable, a seasoned smokejumper. Her cousin, Hannah had been on the team, years ago, so she was a legacy jumper.

Probably never had the probie worries Emily carried around.

Then again, Emily had extra baggage, didn't she?

Nope, not anymore.

And so what if she had to spend the next two weeks hanging out with Mr. Beautiful. She was a professional. Besides, really, she needed to come to her senses.

They lived in two different worlds. There was no way—

What? Now she was dreaming of a relationship? Holy. Cow.

Patrice handed her a brown bag. Emily peeked inside and spotted fries in a Styrofoam container, her burger rolled up in paper.

She slid off the stool and headed to the door.

A guy like Spenser Storm was so far out of her league she'd die of asphyxiation just trying to breathe the same air as him.

The door opened just as she pushed it, and she stumbled forward, tripping.

Hands caught her arms, steadied her. "Whoa. You okay?"

She looked up. Yep, asphyxiation.

Of course, Spenser Storm stared down at her, grinning. He'd washed off the grime from the set, his hair still a little wet and curly behind his ears, strong hands on her arms, those blue eyes caught in hers.

Breathe.

"Wait—you're the woman from today. At the fire." He glanced at her bag. "Is that dinner?"

She nodded. *Words!*

"Shoot. I wanted to buy you dinner."

Oh. She just stood there. "Drink. You said...drink."

Really, Emily?

"Can I...persuade you to eat that here?"

"Here?"

"At the...Hotline? Or, maybe outside on a picnic table. Or...on the sidewalk..."

"Here is good." She practically croaked out the words. *For Pete's sake.*

"Smells good, what is it?" He held the door open for her.

C'mon, Emily, get in the game— "A burger. Fries."

"Perfect." He was still holding the door.

She turned, spotted a magically empty booth and practically fled. From what, she didn't know, because of course, Spenser the Beautiful was on her heels.

For cryin' out loud, pull yourself together.

She slid into the booth, set her bag on the table.

He smelled good, too. Like soap. And he hadn't shaved, so he wore a hint of a beard across his jaw. He'd changed into a simple black T-shirt and jeans, still wore the boots. A regular guy.

If said regular guy was born under a halo of stars, with the angels singing *what a beautiful world.*

"You okay?"

"Yes. Definitely." *Not even a little.* She smiled at him, then grabbed her bag and pulled out the container of fries and the burger. Set the container in front of him. "Want to share my fries?"

"Really? Sure."

She opened the container. They were still hot and crispy, glistening with oil. He grabbed ketchup and poured it into the other side, the upside-down top.

A waitress came over. Looked at Spenser, then at Emily.

Yep. She was sitting here, sharing fries with Quillen Cleveland. Just another day. Whatever.

"I'll have a root beer, and the same burger she has," he said, picking up a fry.

"Cheeseburger with peanut butter and bacon. And I'll have another root beer, too."

The waitress nodded and headed to the kitchen.

"Peanut butter?" he asked, finding another fry.

"My dad had one in Northern Minnesota once, and we've never looked back." She, too, picked up a fry. "So, you okay? Smoke inhalation?"

"Fine. We have a set medic, and he looked me over. And Bucky—he's shaken, but okay."

"Yeah. Poor kid. He'll have some nightmares, I'm sure."

"Hope not, but yeah, it was a scary moment. I can't believe you knew we were in there." He picked up another fry, stirred it around the ketchup.

"I notice things. It's a byproduct of…well, just being aware of your surroundings is a good idea."

He studied her for a second, then nodded. The waitress delivered their drinks, and he lifted his. "To paying attention."

"To rescuing a kid." She raised an eyebrow.

"Right." He smiled then, and it seemed sweet and genuine, like they might be friends.

"That was pretty brave, actually." She cut her burger in half. "Running in after him."

"Yeah, well, I grew up on set, and I know how easy it is to get in trouble."

"Really. I didn't know that."

He cocked his head at her. "What do you know?"

33

Oops. But c'mon, who didn't know Spenser Storm? "The basics. You played the same character for ten years, and the whole world pretty much watched you grow up. And then, I don't know...you sort of disappeared for while? And now you're back, in a western."

He drew in a breath.

Oh, dial it down Em. Don't sound obsessed.

But she *had* left out the crazy court case with a stalker, and the years he was a model for an underwear company—and even that social media fiasco at a comic con a couple years ago.

"At least, that's the talk around town."

He sighed then, almost relieved, it seemed. "Yeah, that's about right. I always get a little worried when I meet new people, like they're going to call me Quillen, ask me to speak Iwoni."

Oh, not her. Ne*ver*. She laughed. It sounded tinny, so she took a sip of her soda. Found her normal voice. "*Can* you speak Iwoni?"

His smile looked almost forced. "Not even a little. I'm so glad I wasn't cast as Tarkon. He had to be practically fluent."

"There are entire clubs devoted to speaking Iwoni."

"Oh, I know. Believe me." He sighed. "Actually, I had a good childhood, growing up on set. It was a family, sorta. After my dad died, they were really all I had."

She nodded, but *that*, she hadn't known. Apparently, *Tiger Beat* didn't discuss those details, preferring his favorite ice cream and current girlfriend. "So, do you like this movie?"

"*The Drifters*? Sure, yeah. It's a remake, sort of,

one of my grandpa's movies—*Men from the High Mountains*."

"I remember that movie. About a couple brothers who save a family from some corrupt ranchers."

"Yep. New music from a guy named Oaken Fox—"

"I've heard of him. He just put out a record."

"Yeah, and of course, Winchester Marshall is the lead, so—"

"So everyone who loves Jack Powers will be lining up at the theater."

"It's got a good shot at a comeback if..." He closed his mouth then, made a face.

"If?"

The waitress—Emily wanted to strangle her—arrived with his burger. "Anything else, sir?"

"No, thanks." He picked up his knife. "This does look delicious."

She took a stab at *If*— "Are you worried about any more accidents on the movie set? Because actually, I'm going to be sort of, there...helping. Just, you know, to make sure—"

"I don't end up trapped in a burning building?" And then he smiled, those blue eyes in hers. "And if I do, you'll be there to save me?"

Definitely. "I'm your girl."

Oh...no. No...no, she did not say—

"Great." He picked up the burger. "Because I need you."

I need you?

Had he lost his ever-lovin' mind?

35

No wonder the woman looked at him with stark panic—he himself fought the urge to put down his burger and bolt.

I need you?

And actually, he did have a real need on his brain—namely, helping him watch over Bucky. After all, she did mention her ability to notice things.

Which is why, as she stared at him, probably with all sorts of predator fears swirling through her mind, he blurted out his big plan. "I've been assigned to watch Bucky…"

Then, while she ate her fries and sort of picked at her burger, he detailed the conversation with Lincoln and Cosmos, and how Bucky had weirdly become his responsibility.

And none of that had anything to do with the weird spurt of happiness that occurred when she'd said she'd be the one on set.

Calm. Down.

"I'll be glad to help you keep an eye on him." Panic receded from her face.

And his chest.

Honestly, the Academy should hand him an Oscar for this last fifteen minutes. Nothing to see here folks. Everything's fine.

He managed to finish off his burger without choking, and washed it down with the root beer while she finished her fries.

"So, how long have you been a firefighter?"

"A hotshot—wildland firefighting. And about three weeks."

He managed to swallow and put the glass down. "Really?"

"Why? Was I that bad?"

"No, you were amazing."

She smiled then, looking away.

Wow, she was pretty. Her blonde hair had a natural curl, and she'd showered and changed into a floral blouse and a pair of jeans, no makeup, but that was okay because it only made her blue eyes stand out.

Frankly, she was a knockout.

Wait... "So, um, am I taking you away from anything right now?"

She raised an eyebrow, then cocked her head.

"I mean, like...is there a hotshot waiting for you?"

She smiled then, and now he really wanted to sprint.

"No," she said. "There's a no-teammate dating policy. And believe me, I'm not into hero types. My parents sort of wrecked me."

"Oh?"

"My Dad runs a SAR team for the Red Cross, and my mom is sort of a national hero—used to work for the NSA, so I grew up with Supers."

"Supers?"

"You know, Superheroes? The kind of people who just have to save the world?" She smiled. "You play them in movies?"

"Not me."

"No, right. Your character '*Saved the Galaxy, One World at a Time*'." She finger quoted the last part.

He laughed then. As did she. And it felt normal and not at all creepy. Not that it should be, but most women he met had this sort of starstruck vibe about them.

She even had a little ketchup on the side of her mouth.

He handed her a napkin, pointed to his mouth.

"Oh." She wiped her mouth, wrinkled her nose. "Could be worse. Could be blood."

"Is that a thing?"

"You hang around me long enough, and...well, I have this ability to attract trouble. You want this last fry?"

"Knock yourself out."

She finished it. He liked a girl who wasn't afraid to eat.

"So, if this is your first gig as a hotshot, what did you do before this?"

She sat back, pulled one leg up in the booth, leaning back against the wall.

Around them, country music played, and he spotted some of the crew at a long table—cameramen, PAs, and the second AD, along with a couple grips.

"Actually, I was in Benson, Washington, at a SAR school over the winter, training a K-9 dog. It didn't work out. Apparently, dogs and I aren't a great fit." She looked away when she said it, then back.

Oh, she'd never make it as an actress. Something—

"Before that, I was in school—psychology and art. But...I didn't graduate."

Again, the faraway look.

"Well, I think being a hotshot might be exactly your game."

She laughed. "We'll see. I'm not sure I'm exactly, well, this was sort of a desperation move."

He picked up his glass. "Here's to desperation."

She met it. "The mass of men leads lives of quiet desperation. What is called reservation is confirmed desperation."

"Impressive."

"Henry David Thoreau. That's what half a psychology degree will get you."

He laughed. "Are you from Montana?"

"Missouri, actually."

"Never been there."

"It's beautiful—lots of forest and rolling hills."

"Family?"

"Two siblings—they're a lot younger than me. You?"

"Only child. My mom died when I was a baby. My dad was a stuntman. He died when I was eight. After that, I was raised by my grandfather."

She seemed to take it all in, new information.

"Like I said, I was on the set a lot, but child actors are only allowed to work six weeks out of the year. So the rest of the time, I was on my family's ranch, the Flying S, near Helena."

"So, you're a real cowboy."

He shrugged, smiled.

"What does Flying S stand for—Storm?"

"Yes, sort of. My great-grandmother's biological father was Guthrie Storme, with an e—baseball player. But she was raised by a pilot as a dad—a man named Truman. So, when she inherited the ranch from her mother—it was called the Hoyt ranch—she renamed it."

"Cattle ranch?"

"Buffalo, actually."

"Your great grandmother sounds interesting."

"She was a famous actress—Chanel Storm."

"Get. Out. Really?"

"Yeah. She was beautiful, and amazing—I didn't realize how amazing until after she died last year, at the age of 94. I had to give her eulogy, and her press secretary wrote it. I discovered so much I didn't know—like the fact that her mother was an actress. Rosie Worth. And that Chanel was a pilot, too. And she was a rock, you know? She stood by people during the McCarthy hearings, and was even good friends with the Reagans. They went to a Billy Graham crusade together, and I remember the President visiting the ranch once. But to me, she was just my great-grandma, who made cookies and loved me, and occasionally sang me to sleep. Coco the Great."

"Why Coco?"

"That was her real name." He finished his root beer.

"Sounds like you two were close."

"We were. She helped me get my head on right after…oh, nothing."

Emily raised an eyebrow.

"I did something stupid after…okay, so I was an underwear model for about a year."

Her eyes widened.

"I know. But I thought it might be a way to get back into acting so, despite my agent's advice, I signed a one-year contract and practically sold my soul."

"Sorry."

"I ended up quitting and going back to the ranch, and I've spent the last three years cowboying."

"But now you're back to acting?"

He sighed, leaned back in the booth, not sure how he'd let her get this far into his life. And it hadn't hurt a bit.

Then again, she wasn't holding a microphone, or a

cell phone for that matter, asking for a selfie, ready to print his every word in a teen magazine.

"I don't know. I was pretty happy on the ranch, and then our foreman, Butcher, died. He'd been our foreman my entire life, so that was rough."

"Especially right after the death of Coco the Great."

"Yeah." He was folding a napkin, smoothing the edges with his knife. "The new foreman, who my grandpa hired, wasn't keen on having the boss's grandson in the bunkhouse, or hanging with the cowboys, so...yeah. I needed a new gig. My agent, Greg, called with a script, and here I am."

She considered him for a long moment, until he finally looked up.

A beat, then, "You don't seem thrilled about it."

"I..." He closed his mouth, made a face.

She put up her hands, clasped them together.

"Activating the Osprey Proxima Nebula."

He stilled. "You watched the show."

She gave him a look. "Three point two billion children grew up watching *Trek of the Osprey* at seven p.m. on Friday nights. Please."

Right. But when she grinned at him, it didn't feel quite so...embarrassing.

Yeah, that's the feeling he had most of the time anyone mentioned Quillen Cleveland, the boy wonder who saved the freakin' universe. Huh. He hadn't realized that until now.

"So? Now that we're in the Nebula...what's the deal with the film?"

"I don't know. It doesn't feel right. It's based off a book, but in the book, the two brothers die. They rewrote the ending so that one of the brothers gets the girl."

"Doesn't sound terrible."

"Yeah, maybe. I don't know. It just feels...off." He saw back. "But what do I know? I'm just a space adventurer."

"Cowboy. Space *Cowboy.*"

He laughed, and it didn't feel terrible. It was after *Trek of the Osprey* that his life went off the rails, so maybe he shouldn't blame it all on Quillen.

"Listen. You grew up creating a massive story. It's in your bones. I have no doubt you know exactly what you're doing. Just trust your instincts a little. I think you were made for this."

He stared at her as the waitress came up and set the bill down on the table.

She reached for it, but he grabbed it first.

"That's more than a drink there, cowboy."

Maybe. But being around her was like a fresh drink of water that he didn't realize he needed.

But suddenly, he was desperately thirsty.

"Thanks again for the rescue today." He met her eyes. *Don't go.*

She scooted out of the booth. "Try not to die between now and tomorrow. I only rescue people once a day, and you're at your quota." Then she winked and walked away.

And he realized that actually, he'd been completely right.

He needed her.

CHAPTER 4

"Tell me everything."

Emily looked up from where she was reading her fire safety manual in her bedroom, the night pressing against her window, the lamp pooling light onto her single bed. She wore her pajama bottoms and a T-shirt and had spent the last hour trying not to let Spenser's crazy words take root in her brain. *I need you.*

Oh boy.

Now, JoJo Butcher stood in her doorframe, eyes big.

"Everything?"

"Please. I saw you sitting with Spenser Storm eating dinner. You two looked cozy." She came in and sat on the bed.

"No." Yes. Maybe—*stop!* "I was asked to be on the set of the movie, just in case they have any more fire emergencies. Spenser wants me to help keep an eye on Bucky Turnquist while I'm there. Apparently, he's a handful."

JoJo untied her shoes. She wore a pair of cargo pants and a T-shirt, her brown hair pulled back into a ponytail. "Yeah, ever since his dad died, he's sort of been the darling of the Jude County Fire Department. He was just a baby when he died, but Gemma's been a single mom ever since—despite her efforts to find a guy here in the postage-stamp town of Ember. She sort of lets him have his way, and admittedly, we do too. So, he can be a bit spoiled."

"How did his dad die?"

JoJo pushed her tennis shoes away and then crossed her legs on the bed. "He was in the terrible accident that took Jock Burns and his team of smokejumpers. They got caught in a fire."

"I heard about that. Their pictures are on the wall in the Hotline."

"Yeah. It was bad. I trained under Jock's daughter, Kate. She's a legend in the smokejumper world, just like her dad. Her cousin, Nova, is on the team. Anyway, Kate married our old Smokejumper Boss, Jed Ransom, and they're in Missoula training a new crew." She pointed to the textbook. "Brushing up on your training?"

"I was thinking if I could give the cast and crew just a small safety course, we'd all be ready in case something else happens."

"I heard it was just overkill on the pyrotechnics teams today."

"Maybe, but the SFX guy walked us through all his explosions—they shouldn't have created sparks, just puffs of fire. Sparks are from ignited material like wood or other charcoal, or even iron or aluminum— none of which was present in the setup of the explosives. So, I'm not sure how it ignited, unless it somehow mixed with the dust material in the squibs they used to show the bullets hitting the building."

"Wow, you've really thought this through," JoJo said. "Maybe you should be an arson investigator."

"No, I'm just trying to figure out how to keep it from happening again." She flipped a page of the book. "And we'll start with some safety training."

"So, I guess that means you'll be on set with Spenser all day, every day, for the next two weeks. What a sacrifice."

"It's no big deal." *I need you.* "We're just friends."

"Until he finds out about this." She patted the blanket that Emily was curled up in, pulling it out to reveal a massive face...of Spenser Storm. She raised an eyebrow.

"It's not a big deal." Emily grabbed it out of her grip. "It came in a gift box when you joined the Stormies."

"The Stormies?"

She closed the textbook. "The Spenser Storm fan club. Listen, I was thirteen, okay? And maybe had a little—"

"Massive."

"Crush on his character, Quillen Cleveland."

"Who didn't? But I didn't join his *fan club.*"

"I was a teenager."

"And yet, you have the blanket, and you were all wrapped up and cozy in Spenser's face."

"Now you're making it weird."

"It is weird. And maybe a little stalkery."

"What? No."

"I'm just saying, there was that court case—some woman who attacked him in his trailer? She went to jail."

Emily blinked at her. "You're a *Trek of the Osprey* fan?"

45

"Of course I watched it. But I did a little Googling on him when I heard they were filming up on Old Henry's land. According to the TMZ article, which they pulled from the testimony, the woman tied him up, made him talk to her in Iwoni, and eventually took pictures of them together while the police tried to negotiate for his release. In the end, he'd promised his eternal love while the police broke down the door. TMZ actually has a pretty in-depth account of the event."

"I know the story. She served five years. It shut down the movie he was making. He never finished it. Too traumatized." She shook her head. "That would have anyone curling into a ball."

"Yeah. Anyway, you might want to get rid of that blanket if he comes over."

"Which would be when, exactly?" She raised an eyebrow. "Even if he did, I'm not going to invite him into my *bedroom*."

JoJo held up her hands. "When he says, *'Hey Baby, let's grab a pizza'* and he comes over and you're eating it outside, under the stars, and he gets chilly and you say, *'Don't worry, I'll get you a blanket.'*"

"Okay, if that ever happens, I'll be sure not to grab the oversized likeness of himself."

"Perf." But JoJo wore a teasing expression in her eyes as she stood up. "And now you get to hang out with him in real life. Maybe you two will be more than friends—"

"Please. But he was nice."

"You were laughing."

"He's funny. And sort of sweet."

"And an actor." JoJo raised an eyebrow. "So watch your heart."

Right.

JoJo headed toward the door.

"What did you say about the Old Henry land?"

"Oh. The land the movie is on is owned by this guy named Henry White. He owns acres and acres of woodland, and I think that old town was actually founded by some great-great-great-great grandfather or something. No one ever sees him—we thought he was dead for a while, but then he'll just show up in town, at the Hotline, or the hardware store, or sometimes in church. Nice old guy, just keeps to himself like he's up there hiding stuff in the woods, or whatever."

She opened the door. Paused. "By the way, if no one told you yet, what you did today was really brave." She looked at Emily. "The first time I was in a fire, I completely froze and had to be rescued by Kate in her fire shelter."

"And now you're a smokejumper."

"Yeah. I had to learn that fear can be healthy if it keeps you awake. But you can't let it into your soul. Can't let it cripple you. I wish I'd learned that earlier. Clearly, you've conquered it."

"Years of therapy."

JoJo raised an eyebrow. "Really?"

"Yeah. I was in a terrible train accident as a kid. Had nightmares for years, along with trauma counseling." She left out the other part, the scariest part, but when was it ever a good time to tell someone you'd been kidnapped? "But mostly that was pure panic back there on the set today."

JoJo laughed. "I'm glad you're on the team."

"Tell that to Miles. I'm still not sure if my assignment to the movie camp isn't a demotion."

"Just keep them from starting any forest fires, and you'll be a hero. You and your blanket have a lovely evening." She winked, then left.

Oh, she hadn't a hope of being a hero. But maybe she could keep tragedy from happening.

I need you.

Yeah, probably not.

But it didn't hurt to dream, right?

You were made for this.

Spenser woke up with Emily's words in his head, and it sort of felt like sunshine poured straight into his soul.

The heat of the words stuck with him as he showered, then opened the tweed blinds while his no-name coffee perked, and as he forewent breakfast in the lounge of the motel. Instead, he hopped on his bike and motored to the set just as the sun broke free of the eastern spread of mountains.

He liked getting to the set early, into his trailer so he could go over the scenes on the call sheet, practice and re-memorize his—today, six—lines, and get into wardrobe before the rest of the team came in.

As he parked, he couldn't help but glance at the house, now charred to the foundation, the chimney in rubble. The barn still stood—that would be fired later in the script. And beyond that, a well, a corral for horses, and a wagon, which was today's victim. The corral was empty, as the woman who ran the local horse sanctuary took them back to her place when they weren't being used in the movie.

He looked away from the house and the what-ifs.

He hadn't quite let his memory linger on those terrifying moments under the house—had relegated the moment to movie magic, something cordoned off in his brain.

Maybe that's why he'd run in—because he hadn't actually considered the danger. But if it weren't for Emily...

He headed over to craft services and grabbed a fresh donut and coffee. Then he turned and searched for Emily.

Maybe she didn't know that most of the cast and crew arrived on set before dawn.

According to the shooting schedule, they had another week of filming at the Winthrop homestead, where Blossom and her son, as well as the Cooper brothers, would bury her husband, then plan their attack on the Irish ranch.

Tomorrow's shoot involved a grass fire, and then, finally, a day later, the barn would be torched before they moved to the old western town for the final sequence of shots.

"Ready for your big scene today?" Win Marshall held his script in one hand, a cup of coffee in the other. Spenser was tall, but Win had him by a half inch. Spenser supposed if he had a real big brother, it might be Winchester Marshall. He had a steadiness about him that he brought to the Jack Powers character.

And now, to the character of Deacon Cooper, reluctant gunslinger.

"The one where I try and fail to talk you out of facing down the Irish gang? Yeah. About that—I feel like the brothers should stick together here. I don't buy Deacon leaving Hawk behind for this gig."

"Even to protect the woman?"

"That's the thing—she's a strong mountain woman with a kid and a dead husband. I'm not sure she needs us sticking around to protect her."

"It's in the book."

"The book was written like forty years ago, and it's a classic that's been remade the same way every time. But I'm not sure it plays to today's female audience. And yes, I can get behind a man protecting the woman he loves, but Hawk doesn't love her yet. He cares more about his brother. Besides, she's in town, and I think we can make a case for her being safe without Hawk there to protect her. It's more believable for two to stand off with six cowboys than one."

"You might have mentioned this at the table read."

Right.

"But you might have a point."

He glanced at Win. "Really?"

"Let me talk to Cosmo." He rolled up the script. "Did you do this a lot with Osprey?"

"Not really. I produced one episode, and that was enough for me. But I did have some say in the finale."

"The one where Quillen finally finds his dad?"

"Yeah. They wanted his dad dead, and I suggested that our entire fan base would murder us if we went that direction."

Win laughed. "Good call. It's one of my favorite episodes. I love a good happy ending." He lifted his hand to Cosmos, who came out of the director's trailer. "See you in makeup."

He took off, and Spenser finished off his donut, watching the sunrise cast upon land. Right now, Kermit would be serving up the guys in the bunkhouse a plate of spicy scrambled eggs, bacon, biscuits, gravy, and home fries.

He headed to makeup. Thirty minutes later, he was grimy, his five-o'clock shadow darkened, his hair gritty.

Win came into the trailer and sat in the makeup chair. "He's working on the shootout, but he liked your changes." Win lifted his chin as Tanya, their makeup assistant, garbed him in a cape. "Next time, though, maybe let's make changes more than just two hours in advance."

Spenser rolled up his script and nodded. Headed over to wardrobe where they put him in freshly laundered, now movie-dusted clothing that smelled great and looked grubby. And in another thirty minutes, he was a gunslinger from the late eighteen hundreds any woman might love.

At least that's what Cosmos was hoping when he handed him the updated pages.

"The AD is working out the blocking." He gestured to the set where Indigo was already talking through the scene with Kathryn Canary.

Gemma crouched next to Bucky as they listened to the instructions.

"Hey."

He turned and didn't stop a smile as Emily walked up to him. She wore her blonde hair back, her canvas fire-retardant pants, a yellow Nomex shirt—a hotshot straight out of casting central. A duffel bag hung from her shoulder.

"Mornin'."

"You look like you've been in a tussle, and it's not even eight a.m."

"We do have a fight scene later today, but no, this is all makeup."

She cupped a hand over her eyes. "Is that Bucky?"

"Yeah. He's in the first scene with Kathryn. Has to mourn his dad. I think I should probably find a game or something to play with Dusty between takes. I lost half my life sitting in chairs waiting for takes."

She looked at him. "Really?"

"Okay, that might be an exaggeration, but I was known for learning every line by every actor in a scene. It wasn't that I was a prodigy—I was bored."

She laughed. "I get that. I'll see if I can entertain him."

"What's in your bag of tricks?"

"Oh. Just some safety gear. A fire extinguisher. A fire-retardant blanket. I thought I'd see if I could run a quick safety seminar."

"Talk to Indigo, the first AD. She's in charge of the shooting schedule." He pointed to the yard in front of the house.

"Right." She turned, looked back. "A fight scene?"

"Just a little scuffle. Gotta dispatch them varmints."

She laughed. It rang inside him as he headed to his trailer.

He stood in front of the mirror, memorizing the new lines. Eight total—so that was a bonus. Tried them out in different variations, different speeds.

The set assistant knocked on his door less than twenty minutes later for a blocking rehearsal. As he came out, he spotted Emily talking with Indigo, who wore a headset, her hands on her hips, her mouth set in a sort of annoyance.

He walked over and caught the end of it.

"We have a tight schedule, Miss Micah. I don't think—"

"Not to interrupt, but I think Emily is just trying to do her job, Indigo."

Indigo raised an eyebrow. Okay, yes, he knew his place, but Spenser still said, "I think after yesterday, maybe we'd all feel safer with a short safety briefing?"

She checked her watch, then turned away and spoke into her headset.

Emily glanced at him. "Thanks." Then her attention diverted to behind him. "Hey!"

He turned. The trailer for the horses had arrived, and a woman was leading the herd of six horses to the corral, all on long leads.

Except one had broken away, skittish as it ran down the street.

Right at Bucky who was crouched in the yard—probably on his mark—playing with a stick.

Sheesh, where was his mother?

Spenser sprinted over, Emily behind him. He whipped off his hat. Planted himself in front of Bucky, waving away the horse.

Out of his peripheral, he spotted Emily as she grabbed the kid, forced him down, her body over his in the dirt.

The animal reared up, and Spenser grabbed at its reins. The horse skittered away, but he approached him, hand up. "Whoa there, pal. Shh."

The animal snorted and backed up, but Spenser stopped, then moved forward again, slowly. He finally put a hand on his withers. "There you go, buddy."

The horse bent his head, sniffed at him.

The woman ran up. "Sorry! Sorry—he's a rascal."

She reached out for the reins. "I'm Sophie Lamb. I run the Valley Ranch."

He handed the reins over. "Not sure he's the right horse for this gig."

"Give him a chance," she said. "He's all bark, no bite."

Tell that to Bucky, but he bit that back.

Then he turned to Emily who had risen, helping up Bucky.

Gemma ran from the craft services tent. "Bucky!" He took off for his mother as Emily brushed herself off.

"You okay?" he asked.

"You sure you want to be an actor and not a stuntman?"

His mouth opened. No, not really. But—

"Just kidding. But that was pretty amazing." She handed him his hat. "Can't wait for the real action to start." She turned and headed back to her dropped duffel bag.

He watched her go, feeling like maybe it already had.

"Storm!"

He turned, and Indigo was motioning him toward her, her face tight. He jogged over.

"What was that?"

He opened his mouth. "The horse got away—"

"Just don't do anything to get hurt, okay? The last thing we need is something shutting down the movie."

He stood there, his mouth open as she walked away. Wait one—

"I knew he was going to be a liability."

The words, spoken into her mic, traveled, hit him in the chest.

He looked up, searching for whom she might be talking to.

His jaw tightened as he saw Cosmos looking at him, then nod and turn away.

You were made for this.

Yes, he was. He tucked on his hat.

His next eight lines just might win him a freakin' nomination.

CHAPTER 5

SHE NEARLY CRIED WATCHING SPENSER, AKA Hawken Cooper, bury a man he didn't know.

Emily stood on the sidelines of the set, trying to study the marked-up script, but every time Hawk dropped to his knees and pulled little Dusty to himself, telling him that *every day the sun rose, his daddy was with him*, she wanted to burst into tears.

For cryin' out loud.

And it didn't help that, from her position, she could also see the screen that showed the camera's takes. Close ups and then wide-shot views, and if the crowd didn't love Hawk Cooper before, they would as he held onto Dusty, tears pooling in his tough- guy eyes.

It didn't help that he'd followed up with so much desperation to avenge Winthrop's death that his brother, Deacon, aka Winchester Marshall, seemed an afterthought.

His fans were going to lose their minds.

Bucky went home at lunchtime, and Spenser spent the rest of the day taking and re-taking a staged-but-so-real scuffle with a handful of bad guys who attacked the ranch. Once, he'd even pulled one of the stuntmen off his horse—an unscripted attack, but one the stunt double easily handled as they rolled in the dirt.

The hits looked so real.

Never mind Winchester Marshall fending off three attackers—but he was Jack Powers, after all, and did most of his own stunts as a rule.

She'd screamed when out of nowhere, one of the big thugs tackled Spenser on set—A big *no, no*, as Indigo pointed out during the first take when she'd gone over to Swen to ask a question. Emily had been put in a big Time Out for that slip up.

But Spenser had rolled out of the attack, and then, suddenly, they cut scene.

And took it again.

And again.

So many angles, so much camera work—some wide shot, some handheld, some down low, many of the cameramen moving, others on a stick.

And no one, not once, actually got hit.

The entire fight was entirely scripted and took up most of the day, with so many takes for power shifts, and close-ups.

At a break, with the sun falling, shadows filling the valley, she listened to Cosmos talk through the different shots and cuts—thirty-one different cuts, so many shots...

"Pretty cool, huh?"

Spenser was drinking a protein shake.

"Very. You're an amazing actor."

He smiled. "Thanks. Great safety briefing."

Oh yeah. She was the real star here. She barely stopped herself from rolling her eyes.

"I loved watching Kathryn trying to get the pin out of the fire extinguisher," he said.

Emily glanced at the actress. She seemed nice, hadn't complained about the safety class. "Indigo hates me."

"She's an AD. Her job is to keep the set schedule moving." He gestured to the shot list. "You figuring out the fire scenes?"

"Yes. I guess there's a prairie fire tomorrow?"

"I think it's in the shot list for today. It's supposed to be after the sun sets, in the darkness, so it'll be a long day."

Right. Noted. "What do you shoot next?"

"I have a scene with Kathryn, in the barn."

"You're the hero, then?"

"Hawk's the hero. Deacon dies in the end."

She nodded and hated the tiny, weird fist in her gut. "It's a kissing scene?"

He made a face and nodded.

"What?"

"I don't know. It seems to me that Kathryn and Win have more chemistry, and frankly, Deacon should be with Blossom, not me. My character is a bit of a rogue. Doesn't have a goal, a plan. He shouldn't get the girl."

"C'mon, even the rogue gets a happy ending."

He gave her a look, and suddenly her entire body turned to fire. She didn't mean—oh, brother.

"At least in this western he does," Spenser said, making it suddenly all better. Then Indigo called him back to the set.

And with the sun casting gold upon the barn, he took Kathryn into his arms and kissed her.

For a guy who'd made a face, he certainly made it look real.

Oh, this was a terrible, awful, no good, very bad idea.

"Emily, did you get a chance to talk to Swen about the prairie fire?" This from the second AD, a man in his late twenties, who spent most of his time running around the set. No wonder he was so thin.

Right. The fire. "I took another look at the schematic, and I think if we position fire extinguishers here," she flipped to her page and pointed to an X she'd penciled in, "and here, and I dig a trench to stop the fire, it should be fine."

"We can computer generate most of the fire. We just need a baseline, and of course, the shot with Blossom watching her entire life burn."

She nodded. It had the potential to be a heart-wrenching scene. "The thing is, we can only burn the field once, so we have to get it right."

"I'll get started on the line." She headed to her truck for her gloves, her Pulaski.

The set designer met her in the field and staked out the fire, then she and a couple of the prop assistants dug a line for the fire. "It jumps this line, we'll grab the canisters." Dirt sank into her pores, and sweat ran a line down her spine.

Night swept down from the mountains, turning the world gray. In the distance, the jagged run of the Kootenai mountains cut across a purple sky. The smell of fresh earth, along with the slightest residue of yesterday's fire, still hung in the air.

Her stomach growled, but she ignored it. *Just keep them from starting any forest fires, and you'll be a hero.*

JoJo's words in her head. In lieu of all the moving

parts on set, her little line in the sand would hardly be called heroic.

And really, she barely knew what she was doing. This was very much starting to look like Commander Dafoe trying to get rid of her.

Swen came out to the field with his crew. "Ready?"

"Yeah, anytime." She stepped back and watched as the grips set up the cameras and the gaffers positioned the lighting, which was more than she'd thought for a fire scene.

Indigo came out with Kathryn to block the scene. No lines, just her standing in front of the flames, an epic shot of loss.

"That line going to be wide enough?" Swen came out to survey the dig.

She'd cut it three feet across, twenty feet long, with two ten-foot lines out to the back.

"There's no wind, and as long as we have the fire extinguishers, we'll be fine." She sounded more confident than she felt. But it was the same line they'd cut during training, and the fire had died in the dirt, so...

And, she'd have her shovel with her, just in case it got out of line.

Swen positioned his people along the side, and she stood off the set as Cosmos came up to check the camera shots. A makeup assistant loosened Kathryn's hair. Even dirty and disheveled, the woman belonged on a magazine cover.

They ran lines one more time, then Indigo raised her hand. "Quiet on the set!"

Emily didn't see Spenser anywhere, but her gaze was on Swen, who depressed the radio frequency detonator, and in the distance, fire alighted against the night.

The cameras had dropped low, getting an upward shot, and Kathryn stepped into it, staring out at the fire.

It grew fast, the flames lengthening, crackling, whirling, and twisting in the night.

Mesmerizing.

Kathryn faced the inferno, her expression resolute, tears cresting down her face.

Emily could feel it—the desperation, the loneliness, the fear—

And just like that, for a second, she smelled creosote burning, heard the shouts and screams lifting into the night, felt herself swept into chaos—

"Cue wind," said Indigo quietly and yes, Emily heard it, but the panic was still winding through her, finding her lungs, cutting off her breathing, shutting her down—

In the darkness, just beyond the fire, a prop assistant turned on a fan.

The flames burst to life, doubling, wicked and bold—

Kathryn screamed, stepping back, about to run. Sparks caught her dress.

And just like that, Emily was back. "Drop!"

She burst into the scene, grabbed Kathryn and shoved her down.

The woman fell, and Emily scooped up dirt and flung it at Kathryn's dress. Kathryn rolled over, backing up, still screaming, the flames sizzling.

"Roll!" Emily picked up more dirt, showered it on her.

Then she dropped the shovel and simply landed on the actress, her gloves snuffing the flames.

A flame blanket landed on them, and she grabbed it and rolled it into Kathryn's skirt.

The woman was still screaming.

Emily turned to her, grabbed her arms. "Stop moving. Stop!"

Kathryn looked at her, breathing hard. Tears now real.

"You're okay. You're okay. It's out. Breathe."

Kathryn's eyes fixed to hers.

Then Swen swooped in with the set medic, and hands pulled Emily away. She stumbled back as more assistants poured in, crowding them.

Someone came with a stretcher, but Kathryn was up, pulling up her burned dress to assess the damage. Miraculously, her legs, covered in tights, seemed unscathed. Still, the medic threw the blanket around her shoulders and led her away.

Emily just stood in the darkness, trying to catch her breath.

"You might be the worst firefighter I've ever met."

She looked up. Swen stood there, also breathing hard. "Me?"

"You said this line would hold—the fire jumped the line."

She blinked at him. "Are you kidding me? Someone started a fan! Do you know what wind *does* to a fire?"

A muscle ticked in his jaw. "Get off my set and never come back." Then he turned and walked away.

She stood in the field, watching as the prop assistants killed the fire with the fire extinguishers, the words echoing in her head.

Just keep them from starting any forest fires, and you'll be a hero.

Fine. Whatever. Not even a surprise, really.

She put the shovel over her shoulder and headed to the parking lot, not looking back.

Probably she should just keep going, all the way to Missouri.

"Emily!"

Spenser saw her stalk to her truck—it bore the logo of the Jude County Hotshots—throw her shovel in the back, get in, and in a second, she'd spun out of the lot, dirt spitting.

He'd been off set, in his trailer cleaning up when the action started, had emerged only when he heard the screams.

Watched as Emily again ran right into danger, threw herself on Kathryn—and to his mind—saved the woman's life.

Or at least her stockings. Because as he stood, watching in horror, Kathryn shrugged off help and marched to her trailer, slamming the door behind her.

The medic was still knocking when Emily ran from the field.

Swen wore murder on his face.

Now, he ran up to Swen, grabbed the man's arm. "What happened?"

"That stupid girl let the fire get out of hand and nearly burned down the entire set."

Spenser stared at him. "This isn't on her. You're in charge of Special Effects. Get it right."

Swen rounded on him. "I think maybe the

Underwear Model might need to keep his mouth shut. Do your job, let me do mine." He shook out of Spenser's grip.

But Spenser had nothing anyway. Underwear Model? Seriously?

Swen marched away.

"Let him go, Spense."

He turned, and Winchester stood there. He'd taken off his makeup, showered, changed clothes. Swung his keys in his hand.

"This was not her fault."

Win considered him a moment. "You'll have to talk about that with Cosmos. But I think I heard him fire her."

And Spenser didn't know why that sort of hit him in the gut, why he turned and headed toward the Director's trailer. Shouting spilled out of the half-closed door. "Do better, Swen! Did you tell her that you were going to turn on a fan?"

"It's in the script—all Caps. Her hair *blows back*."

"Maybe she doesn't know how to read a script!"

"Then she shouldn't be on set!"

"You should have put it in the Scene Breakdown sheet!" This again from Cosmos.

Silence. Then, tightly, from Indigo, "Can she even read a Scene Breakdown sheet?"

Ho-kay. Spenser didn't even knock, just took the stairs and opened the door.

Both men and Indigo looked at him.

"So, pretty much all of Montana can hear you, but I have an idea."

Swen folded his arms.

Cosmos took off his glasses and ran a finger and thumb against his eyes.

"I go over the script with her. I'll teach her how to read it." He looked at Indigo. "And the Scene Breakdown sheet."

"Too late," Swen said. "I already fired her."

"Well *unfire* her," Spenser said and looked at Cosmos.

Cosmos held up a hand. "Since Linc is not here, that is my call. And if we want to stay in the good graces of the locals, my guess is that it's probably best to play well with others." He looked at Spenser. "You want to get her back?"

In every sense of the word. "Yes."

Swen shook his head and turned away, but Spenser ignored him and headed back to his trailer. He grabbed his keys and helmet and found his bike.

Calm. Down.

He didn't know why Swen's words had lit a fire inside him. He couldn't care less about the underwear comment.

But something the man said to Emily had really hurt her, the way the rocks peeled out under her tires. And weirdly, that hurt *him.*

Sheesh, he barely knew her. But something... there was something between them.

Something he didn't want to let go of.

He kept it under the speed limit into town—too many dirt roads—and finally spotted the lights of Ember glittering in the valley.

And that's when he realized he didn't know where she lived. But she was a hotshot. And all the hotshots hung out at the Hotline Saloon.

Music pulsed into the night, and when he pulled up, took off his helmet and went inside, a band played in the back section of the restaurant.

He spotted the only other firefighter he recognized, a guy who'd been at the scene that day, and went over to him. He was tall, bald, a few scars on his neck, but otherwise a nice-looking guy who wore a T-shirt, the words LCC Community Church on the front. "Hey. Remember me?"

The man smiled. "Think so."

Right. "I'm looking for Emily Micah. Do you know where she lives?"

"With me. I'm JoJo." A brunette came over, pretty, curvy, in her late twenties. "Just up the road a couple blocks. Give me your phone, and I'll grab the GPS."

He pulled his cell from his pocket, unlocked it, and handed it over.

"I'm Charlie." He motioned to the bald guy. "That's Houston." Charlie had salt and pepper hair and wore a JCHS T-shirt.

"Don't get cold," JoJo said as she handed back the phone, and he frowned at her. It was about a hundred degrees outside.

Whatever. "Thanks."

He left and used the phone to guide him to a nearby neighborhood. The house sat in a tiny lot — clearly a rental — but painted white, with a light over the small front porch.

He parked his bike, took off his helmet, drew in a breath, and headed to the door.

Music played inside. *Don't stop believin'.*

A Journey fan. Interesting. He knocked. No answer.

Knocked again. "Emily?"

The music was too loud. Shoot. He debated, then touched the doorknob.

Unlocked.

Here went nothin'. He pushed open the door.

Stilled.

Not a big house—the living room connected right to the kitchen, a couple sofas in front of a coffee table that faced a flat screen. In the kitchen, a table was shoved against the wall, maybe to make a dance floor, because in the middle, stood Emily.

She wore a pair of leggings and a T-shirt, her back to him, singing into a wooden spoon for all she was worth. "Hold...on, Streetlight, People—" Then she turned. "Oh! *Oh!*"

Then she just threw the spoon across the room. It clattered over by the sofa, bounced onto the floor.

She stared at him as her background music blared.

Then she whirled around, went to the stove, and shut off the flame.

Stayed there, her back to him, just breathing.

"Emily?"

"Uh. Hi."

"Hi."

Silence.

"Sorry to break up the Karaoke. Where do I sign up? I do a great rendition of 'A Thousand Miles,' but if it's theme night, I can pull off a decent 'Eye of the Tiger.'"

A beat.

"You really know 'A Thousand Miles?'"

"Making my way downtown, walking fast, faces past—"

She turned, held up her hand. "Okay, that's pretty good. You don't make it as an actor, maybe you try singing."

"Oh no, I'm going straight back to underwear." Shoot, she'd been crying, evidenced by the red in her eyes, her bright cheeks. "You okay?"

She looked away, then spotted her spoon on the floor and went over to pick it up. "I was fired. But you know, it could have been worse. I could have burned down the entire county, not to mention an A-list actress."

"She's hardly A-list."

She stared at him. "Okay, so I wasn't a fan of her last movie, but certainly she's up there with say, Lauren Graham."

It took just a second. "Gilmore Girls?"

"Listen, *Trek of the Osprey* was finished. What did you expect of me?"

He liked a girl who could laugh at herself. "You're not fired."

"Hello. Were you there? Did you miss the screaming? I threw *dirt* on the leading actress. Even if she's not an A-lister, there has to be consequences."

And it was how she said it...he took a step toward her—

"Don't come near me. I'm still radioactive."

Oh. He held up his hands. "Please. Listen. *You're not fired.*"

She gave him a look.

"Really. Not lying." He held up three fingers.

"Don't give me that. You were never a boy scout."

He put his hand down. "How did you know that?"

"No one is actually a boy scout. Sheesh. Swear to me on the Star of Elianna."

His mouth opened. "Seriously?"

"You want me to believe you?"

"Please. I'll swear on *anything* else. Grapthar's Hammer—"

"Nope."

"For crying out—okay, I swear on the brightest star of the Omega Galaxy, Star of Elianna, that what I heard is honest and true."

"I'm not fired."

"I just swore on—"

She held up her hand. Sighed. "Really?"

"Yes. If you want the job. But there are conditions."

"Conditions?" She went to the stove and picked up the pot. "It'll have to wait until I finish my overly cheesy cry-me-a-river macaroni and cheese."

She poured water into the colander, and noodles fell into the pot. "Grab me the heavy cream—it's in the fridge."

He spotted a pile of grated cheddar cheese on a cutting block as he opened the fridge. "This is serious macaroni and cheese."

"For a seriously bad day."

He handed her the cream. She'd poured the noodles back into the pot, added the cheese and now poured in the cream and stirred. "I might just eat it out of the pot. Do you want a fork or spoon?"

"Spoon?"

"Good choice." She plunked down a wooden spoon from a crock, then a hot pad, and carried the pot out to the living room.

He came over to her. "Do I get to sit by you?"

She raised an eyebrow.

"Because of the radioactive part?"

"Take your chances."

He sat down, and she handed him the spoon as she put the pot on the table. Sat back.

"Aren't you eating?"

"I lost my appetite. Sometimes I just make the food and then stare at it."

He had nothing for that.

"It's a therapy technique. Sometimes you just have to go for what feels good, and then, maybe, before you let it take over, you just see it for what it is. A tool to help you get to the deeper issue."

"Which is?"

"Maybe Swen is right. Maybe I'm not cut out to be a hotshot. Maybe I really stink at this."

"You made it through training, right?" He dug into the macaroni. "This is really good."

"I know. I've perfected it. Sharp Cheddar and Gouda. And just because I made it through training doesn't mean I'm not going to crash and burn—look at today."

"Why would you—"

"Because I have PTSD."

He stopped mid-bite. Looked at her. "What?"

"Ten seconds before Blossom nearly burned to death, I was in my six-year-old body climbing my way out of a train crash. If I hadn't been triggered, maybe I would have seen the fire jump the line."

He put down his spoon. Leaned back. "You were in a train crash."

"When I was six years old. But that's the tip of the Titanic-sized iceberg. And before we dive into this, let me say that you're free to get up and leave any time this feels too much."

"Give me a try."

She smiled. "My mom was a spy, on the run for

the first five years of my life with information that revealed corruption in the government. They sent an assassin to kill her, and in the scuffle, the train was derailed. Then, I was lost in the forest, chased, and kidnapped. And after that, held for ransom and nearly watched my mom die. Then, she married the man she loved, they had two kids, and we all lived happily ever after. Hand me my spoon."

He picked up her wooden spoon and she leaned over, took a bite. "Yeah, that's one of my better batches." She set the spoon down. "Now I'm full."

"Me too. So much to unpack there. I don't know where to start. Maybe at the end with *'and we all lived happily ever after.'*" He raised an eyebrow.

"Oh, I'm still figuring out that part. When I was ten, my parents took us on one of those day trains in Colorado, and I had a complete panic attack, meltdown, clinging to the seats, screaming. So, that began many beautiful years of therapy." She smiled.

He didn't. "I was held hostage by a fan."

She looked at him.

"I'm not comparing situations. I was a grown adult, but I came out of the bathroom of my trailer and a woman was there, with a gun, and she…was a little zealous about wanting me to marry her. And when I say marry, I mean in the Biblical sense of the word."

"Oh."

"Yep. Nothing happened—I mean, she was holding me at gunpoint, so I'm not sure what she expected, but it was about the two most terrifying hours of my life. She was found mentally unstable and sent to prison, but I sort of fled moviemaking and went to college."

"And then to underwear."

"My own personal iceberg." He touched her hand then. "My therapist was my great-grandma. The song she used to sing to me? "It Is Well with My Soul." It's a hymn, and it's about how, deep inside, you can be well—solid, strong, healthy—even though the world is on fire around you. I'm still trying to figure that out, but I do know that what I saw of you says that despite everything you've gone through, deep inside, you're brave. And smart. And have good instincts. You saved our B-list actress today, and maybe the entire movie. And frankly, we need you."

There, he said it again, or at least a variation. *We need you.* And this time he meant it.

She sighed. "What's the condition?"

"I have to teach you how to read a script. And a Scene Breakdown sheet. If you'd known how to do that, you would have known that all Capital Letters always means a Prop or a Shot direction. Which meant—"

"Her Hair Blows in the Wind required a fan."

"Yep."

She sighed. Looked at him. "Fine. But I have my own condition."

"What's that?"

"I'm going to need to hear you sing the entirety of 'A Thousand Miles.'"

He grinned and picked up his spoon.

CHAPTER 6

"SOMETHING GOING ON BETWEEN YOU TWO?"

The question came from Kathryn, who walked up holding a bottle of water. She wore her hair in an elaborate bun, a clean dress, nothing of the trauma of a couple nights ago on her face.

But maybe, like him, she'd learned how to compartmentalize.

"Me and Bucky?" Spenser stood back as Bucky swung the lasso around his head. He'd set up a chair from the craft services tent in the field behind the set and had grabbed a lasso from the prop department, spent the last couple days teaching Bucky how to spin the rope above his head and throw it over the top of the chair. "You're getting it, kid, good job."

"No. You and the Hotshot."

The Hotshot.

His gaze went to Emily, standing behind the cameras, holding a fire extinguisher. Not a high chance that the squibs they'd set to pop in the saloon would result in a flame, but now that she knew how to read a script, and the Scene Breakdown sheet, she'd been hyper vigilant.

Swen largely ignored her, but frankly, everyone felt a little better having a firefighter on set.

"No. We're just friends. I taught her how to read a script."

"You two are spending a lot of time together." Kathryn took a sip of water, then turned to watch the scene behind them playing out. "A little off set romance happening?"

The Deacon character had donned the sheriff's tin now and was embroiled in a heated conversation with the villain, Duke Irish. In a moment, a few of Irish's cronies would show up and spatter the street with bullets.

"Really, she's just here doing her job."

"Yep."

"What?"

"I just see the way she looks at you."

"What way is that?"

"Like you're made of stardust. Are you sure she's not a crazy fan?"

He frowned at her. "What? No. Not even a little. Great throw, Bucky."

Bucky looked over at him, grinned, his two front teeth missing. "Thanks, Spenser."

He turned back to Kathryn. "She watched the show, once upon a time. Everyone did. Doesn't make her a crazy fan."

She raised an eyebrow. "Just be careful."

He gave her a look.

"Don't get me wrong. I like her. She not only saved me from being burned, but yesterday, we hung out a little. She's nice. Easy to be around."

Yes, that was it. She was easy to talk to.

Easy to laugh with.

Easy to sing karaoke with. And probably that was the something between them. She was easy to be around. Made him feel like…himself. Which was strange because he was still trying to figure out who that was, really.

But he wasn't *falling* for her.

"Spense, I hate to be the one to say this, but you need to think about your future. After this—what? Hollywood, or back to the ranch? If you're headed back to a normal life, that's one thing. But if you have your eyes set on Hollywood, you need to be careful. You don't need a repeat of—"

"I know."

"Fine. You know what it takes to make it. Focus. Commitment. And, you have to be able to trust the people around you. Which means being careful about who you let into your world."

He blinked at her. "Emily is not a crazy fan stalker. She's a normal person. If anything, I need to protect *her* from *my* world."

"Also my point—she might not belong in your world. This isn't real—it's a movie set. Remember that."

She walked away, Spenser wordless in her wake, just as the set PA, a skinny guy named Gil, came up with a clipboard and today's shooting schedule. "I need to grab Bucky for a quick blocking rehearsal."

Spenser walked over to Bucky, who surrendered the rope. "Can we do that again?"

"Tomorrow, probably. I think your day is done after the scene in the livery stable."

He spotted his mom, Gemma, heading over to grab his hand. Nice woman, really. Unfamiliar with set life, however, and maybe he shouldn't be so hard on her. Not easy to keep an eight-year-old quiet or trapped in his trailer all day.

Bullets—the squibs—shot off, and nearby, in the corral, horses spooked. They started to run in circles, and for a second, he was back on the street, calming the horse, Emily protecting the kid.

They did make a good team.

On the street, Win was a pro, dodging bullets, firing back his own. A cowboy rode by, fell off his horse. The other continued on, out of town. Win came out, looked after him, then ran to the sheriff's office.

"Cut!" Cosmos shouted.

The cowboy on the street didn't get up, and in a moment, the team medic ran out to him. Spenser headed over to the set.

The stuntman sat up, touched his shoulder, grimacing.

"It looks dislocated." Emily came to stand beside him.

"Yep," Spenser said. "Comes with the job. It happened a couple times to my dad. He had this trick on how to reset it. How are you doing?"

She was cute today, dressed in her hotshot uniform. She wore a handkerchief over her blonde hair, a pair of sunglasses. He didn't know why, but he found it a little hot.

If a guy were noticing that sort of thing.

"Great. Indigo spoke to me today."

"Really?"

"Yep. Said, 'get out of the way'. But then she looked at me and gave me a sort of grimacy smile, so that's good, right?"

"First ADs are the bad guys. They have a lot on

their shoulders." On the street, the stuntman got up, grimaced, headed off set.

"That's right. You said your dad was a stuntman."

"Yeah. A legend, really. He died in an accident on set. But he saved one of the child actors, so he was a hero."

"I'm so sorry. That's rough."

"Yeah. For a while, I really wanted to be like him. A real hero, not someone who just acts like a hero."

"Maybe being a hero isn't just doing, but inspiring people *to* do. I think there were plenty of kids inspired by Quillen Cleveland's determination to find his father."

He looked at her. "Really?"

"Yeah. You made perseverance so cool. Or at least, Quillen did. And then when he found his dad, it was...awesome."

"That was my idea. The writers wanted him dead."

She made a face. "Talk about trauma. Three billion sci-fi fans in counseling."

He laughed. "I doubt that."

"Don't."

He looked at her. That was another thing he liked about Emily—she somehow knew how to make him feel like he might actually be the guy people saw on the screen. Brave. Smart. Heroic.

"I think you're right. I might have been in counseling myself if we hadn't found him."

She nodded. "Maybe in a way, Quillen's quest to find his dad was your own quest to say goodbye to yours."

He stared at her, blinking, the words finding a home. "Yeah. I...hadn't thought about that."

On set, Bucky and Indigo walked over to the livery stable attached to the corral. The horses were still spooked, but Indigo seemed to not notice, moving Bucky into place. He was only supposed to stand in the door, watch Deacon saddle his horse. Ask him where he was going, to which Deacon said something heroic, and then Dusty would watch as he rode away.

But from the corral, a horse reared up, still agitated.

Just like that, Bucky dropped to a crouch, his hands over his ears, and screamed.

Indigo stared at him in horror.

Gemma squatted next to him, her hands on his arms, stricken.

Emily took off. She ran over to Bucky, still screaming, and crouched next to him. She put her hand on his back and leaned in.

Spenser had followed her and now heard her voice, calm, quiet. "You're safe, Bucky. You're safe."

He'd stopped screaming, but his breaths fell over each other, too fast. Behind them, the horses whinnied, snorted, fidgety.

"Pick him up, Spense," Emily said, and he glanced at Gemma, who nodded.

"Can I pick you up, Bucky?" he asked. Bucky nodded.

He swooped the kid into his arms, and Emily directed him inside the livery stable, away from the commotion. The place had been stocked with fresh straw for the shot, and he set Bucky down, sat with him.

Emily crouched in front of him. Put her hands on his shoulders. "Okay, breathe with me, Bucky. In.

And out. In…and out. This will pass. You're going to be fine. You're safe."

Bucky looked up at her, those big green eyes in hers. Gemma crouched beside her, rubbing his back.

"You're doing great. How about telling me five things you can see."

He looked up. "A horseshoe."

"Good. Something else?"

"My mom."

"Mmmhmm."

"A saddle."

"Good."

"A hay bale." He looked at Spenser. "Spenser?"

"Yep, Spenser is here." Now she too looked at him, met his gaze, something sweet in it.

And his heart simply turned over. *We need you.*

"Okay, some smells?"

"Horse poop." He made a face. His breath had slowed.

"Manure. Good. Anything else?"

"Dirt. And Spenser."

"Yeah, Spenser does smell."

"I don't smell."

"He does smell. Like dirt and sweat and maybe even horse poop. Yuck." She held her nose.

"Hey!"

Bucky laughed.

"What do you hear?"

The thump of his heartbeat? The rushing sound of something slipping out of his control?

"Birds."

"Birds. Good. Anything else?"

Cosmos had come into the barn, along with Lincoln and Indigo, and even Winchester.

"Horses," he said quietly, his breath shivering.

"Yes, horses. The horses are locked in the corral, where they're staying. They won't hurt you. You're safe. Right, Spenser?"

"Right." He looked at Cosmos. "What if I came in the barn with him? I know Hawk is supposed to be with Blossom right now, but maybe I come in with Bucky and we watch Deacon ride out together?"

Cosmos' mouth tightened, but he nodded. "That could work." He came up to Bucky. "You think you could do this scene if Spenser is here?"

Bucky wiped his cheeks. Nodded. "Can she stay?" He pointed to Emily. "I like her."

Yeah, what the kid said.

Cosmos smiled. "Sure."

Emily held out her hand and Bucky took it as he climbed out of the straw. Then he held the other out to Spenser.

He took it. And they walked out of the barn together.

A team.

That's all.

For sure he completely ignored Kathryn Canary, standing in the door frame, shaking her head.

"I heard you were a bit of a hero today on the set."

Emily looked up from where she sat at the table in the office of the Jude County Fire team, drawings spread out in front of her. She held a red pen, her glass of iced tea sweating onto a coaster.

Outside, the sun had set, the moon had risen, the stars sprinkled the tarmac of the fire station with a dusting of silver. A cool night, given the heat of the day, a slight breeze ticking up.

It took a second to register Conner's words. "I don't know what you're talking about."

He wore a pair of gray canvas pants, a T-shirt with JCHS on the breast, his dark blond hair cut short for the season. "Liza was picking up ribs tonight for dinner and said she talked to Gemma, who was also in getting food. Said that Bucky had some sort of meltdown on set."

"Just a smidgen of PTS. He was scared by a horse on set a few days ago, and I think he just freaked out. He'll be okay."

Helped, too, that Spenser had been there, helping her calm him. She might find herself breathing more calmly with Spenser around too.

Or not. Because something about the way he looked at her…

As if he liked her…really liked her.

Not acting.

But really, who knew?

"She said you did some cool technique to calm him down."

"The Five-Four-Three-Two-One. It's actually a focus technique I learned from a trauma specialist. Helps to focus on your surroundings, calm your breathing. Remind you that you're safe."

"You're pretty good at that."

"Psychology degree. And years of field work." She winked.

"Sounds like assigning you to the movie set wasn't a terrible idea."

She shrugged and smiled.

"And that smile has nothing, I'm sure, to do with

the fact that you and Spenser Storm seem to be friends."

She looked at him.

"JoJo said he came over the other night."

"Your spy network is exhaustive."

"How else am I going to file my reports to your father?"

Her mouth opened.

He held up his hand. "Kidding. Mostly." But he winked. "Still, anything going on between you and Storm? Do I need to go up there and have a what-are-your-intentions Uncle chat?"

"Now I'm going to have nightmares, thanks."

He laughed.

"For the weekly report, you can tell my father that nothing is going on. We're friends."

Conner raised an eyebrow, arms folded.

"Please. He's a movie star."

"Whose life you saved."

"You think he's my friend because he feels guilty?"

His eyebrows raised. "What? No. Just—he's not a superhero. He's a regular guy, that's all. Can't he fall for a pretty hotshot?"

She rolled her eyes.

"What?"

"It's just...no. He makes me laugh. And he's charming, but...no." Although today, when he'd taken Bucky's hand, then looked at her, something felt...right.

Real.

Safe.

She'd sort of hoped he'd motor up to her house tonight, but when she left, the light was burning in his trailer, so maybe he was rehearsing.

And really, they were just work friends. Nothing more.

Even with his rather beautiful rendition of "A Thousand Miles."

"Well, maybe remember that he's going to finish up this movie and head back to Hollywood, so don't lose your heart to him."

"Oh, it's way too late for that." But she winked at him. "However, I do promise not to hop on the back of his motorcycle and ride away into the horizon."

"He has a motorcycle?"

"Yeah, a vintage looking Victory. Very hot."

"I think I'll keep that out of my *daily* report." He reached out and flipped a chair around, sat on it. "What are you working on?"

"I'm just trying to figure out what equipment we need for the barn fire tomorrow. I'm glad you're still here—I think we need the water truck to come out, and maybe a team of five, at least." She pointed to marks on the drawing. "They can stand here and still be out of the camera's view. The fire is mostly smoke, and the main blaze will be in two drums set inside the door—they're not actually burning the barn down. But it is a barn with straw and hay, and I'd like the team to wet it down really well before the fire starts. And, of course, to be on hand if anything goes south."

Conner moved the schematic toward him, perused it. "So, these are the fire drums?"

"Yeah. It's supposed to look like there's fire coming from the main doors—our hero runs inside to rescue Dusty. I'm not sure he's going to be the one in the fire after today. I think they'll run the scene without the fire, and then do it with the fire, and composite them together. The magic of film making."

"You sound like a pro."

"No. Just a lot of time listening to Swen and his team. They have it largely under control. I'm just wanting some backup. After the near miss at the field—"

"What near miss?"

"Long story, but a grass fire nearly got out of control. We stopped it, but Swen is taking no chances with the barn fire. I am learning a lot, though. Shooting a movie is tedious, long hours and lots of retakes. And just because it's acting doesn't mean the trauma isn't real. It might even be more real because they know they are acting, but they experience the same emotions as if they weren't—otherwise it wouldn't feel real on the set. The difference is, they don't get to deconstruct it. They have to shrug it off."

"You sound like a therapist."

"I talked with Kathryn Canary yesterday for a long time about her different roles. She once zip-lined off a tower of some historic German church only to have the brakes fail. Scared her to death. And then she was nearly burned up on the set. Clearly, bad things happen to her, too."

He frowned at her. "Bad things."

"You know. The train crash. The kidnapping. You were there."

"Emily, that was nearly twenty years ago."

She lifted her shoulder. "I'm just always aware that around the next corner, disaster waits."

His mouth opened. Closed. "No wonder you're twirling your hair." He reached up and touched a snarl where she'd worked her hair into a knot. "Next thing you know, you'll be yanking it out."

"That was one semester, in seventh grade."

"Right after your little brother was born."

She reached up, touched the rat's nest. Made a face.

"Emily. Fear is believing that evil is in control of your life. Your future. But I happen to know that you are a woman of faith. And faith says that God is the one in charge of your life."

"I know." She patted her head. "I just want to be prepared."

He considered her for a moment. "I keep running through that incident, a week ago, when you ran toward the fire to rescue Bucky and Storm. And it was brave, for sure. But also, incredibly impulsive. That kind of behavior is dangerous—not just for you, but for your crew."

"It was an instinct."

"I get that. But knowing you—it's also you kicking your fear in the teeth."

"Of course I am. I'm Lacey Montgomery's daughter. I'm not going to let fear win."

"Fear wins when it makes you do something stupid. When it makes you act outside of wisdom. God does not give us a spirit of fear, but of power and love and *a sound mind*."

"Listen. Fear shows up, and I can't let it hold me hostage. I have to fight back."

"Or, you let God fight your battles. You rebuke the fear, don't let it control you. When you live in trauma and in fear, you live outside the presence of God in your life. And without God, your soul is not well. Lies win. And that's when we make bad decisions."

Conner pushed the papers back to her.

"You experienced a trauma, that's for sure. But

you are not a victim anymore. You are a survivor. More than that, you're a daughter of God, in His hands. And that changes everything. Prepare, but don't live in fear."

"I'm just doing my job."

"I'm glad you are on the team, Emily. You passed training without a hiccup. But I can't quite figure out why you're doing this, and not, I don't know…"

"Working for my dad on his SAR team? Yeah, that's easy. Because he doesn't want me."

Conner's mouth opened, and oops, probably she shouldn't have said that to his best friend.

"Emily, I —"

"Sorry. I shouldn't have said it like that. I just mean…he thinks I'm going to get hurt." She lifted her shoulder. "Now who is living in fear?" She smiled.

He didn't. "Your dad wants you on the team, Emily. But I happen to know that he thinks that God has something else for you."

Emily drew in a breath. "Shouldn't I be the judge of that?"

"Should you?"

A beat.

"What's in charge here—fear, or faith? Trust or run?"

She said nothing. Frankly, she'd never even considered the question.

"I'm not saying you're not brave, Emily. In fact, you're one of the bravest people I know. But maybe, there's something deeper inside that you haven't yet confronted."

"Now who's the therapist."

"Right. Well maybe it's just your godfather sharing with you a little of what he's learned in his life." He pressed a hand to her shoulder. "I also promised your dad that you wouldn't get hurt. So, please, don't make me a liar."

"I won't."

He got up. "I'll send half the crew up with you tomorrow morning. Keep the movie from burning down the town."

"Thanks, Uncle Conner."

He smiled, then headed back to his office.

She stacked the papers, then put them in her backpack and headed outside.

The moon was up and full and casting down on the parking lot. *'What's in charge here? Fear or Faith?'* And for a moment she was six years old, hiding behind a tree, hearing a voice calling to her in the darkness, asking herself the very same question. Trust or run?

The problem was, the *secret* was, once upon a time, she had trusted.

And that was the terrible truth she couldn't seem to wedge out of her heart.

What happened when you trusted...and your world still turned into a nightmare?

CHAPTER 7

THEY HAD AN AUDIENCE.

"Who are all these people?" Emily asked Indigo as she outlined her burn prevention plan. Three men stood at the edge of the set wearing suits, one in cowboy boots, their hands in the pockets of their dress pants, mouths pursed, eyes watching the set behind their aviator sunglasses.

She and Indigo stood in front of the barn. An old, weathered barn that was more tinder than structure. One wrong spark and the entire thing would be an inferno.

"Investors. And an insurance man. The production company heard about the house fire and are concerned."

"No one is going to burn to death on my watch."

Indigo looked at her, gave a half smile. "You do look the part today. You're very geared up. Helmet, scarf, water bottle, ax—"

"Pulaski."

"What's in the leg pocket?"

"Fire shelter. We have to carry one at all times."

"Maybe having you and your team on set will

calm down the money. Get your team in place—we'll shoot as soon as Swen is ready."

Emily walked to the back of the barn and waved to Swen. "The barn is hosed down!"

He and his team had spent most of the day setting up the propane tanks and hoses that led to the drums that would ignite the fire in front of the barn doors. The effect would be spectacular if it went off the way he'd shown it to her on the animated mock-up.

And, Swen hadn't given her any guff about hauling in her team to stand by. Nor wetting down the barn and hay and straw inside the building. Not with the fire index in the area high, a slight wind bullying its way into the valley.

"Where do you want us?" Houston James asked. He and Dakota had arrived this morning, had watched as Bucky ran his scene inside the barn, then outside as Hawk ran in and saved him.

She just about had to sit on her heart, stop it from weeping when he set Dusty down—who was doing a superb job of crying—and looked him in the eyes and told him not to be afraid. All while covered in soot and grime, and definitely the guy she wanted to run to in a fire, or really anywhere, to save her. *Maybe don't lose your heart to him.*

Ha. Ha. Ha. Oh, she was pitiful.

He even came over to her afterwards, pushed his hat up with one finger and said, "I talked Cosmos into adding that line about not being afraid. Felt like it gave Hawk more humanity. But now...I don't know."

"It was great." Never mind the girl melting into a puddle at your feet. "I think it works."

Now who was the actor?

Next, they'd film the scene where they fired the

barn, and while Deacon Cooper comforted Blossom, Hawken Cooper, aka a stuntman, ran inside to save Dusty (who wasn't there.) And, of course, back out.

All while *not* burning to death. No problem.

At least that was her goal.

"I need you in the back of the barn, ready to put out any sparks that might ignite outside the window," she said now to Houston. "Dakota, you're on the other side."

She'd put Charlie and Orion on the hose in front of the barn, just a few feet away from the camera, close enough to douse the fire if it should spark any grass, although she'd had the crew cut a line in front of the barn too.

Not that she was in charge—Conner had driven up in his truck with the team, briefed them all, then headed back to town to chase down a spot fire with the Trouble Boys and the rest of the team. Apparently, something had started up by the hospital in Snowhaven. But he'd handed her the reins and gone over the goal with them.

No fires, everybody stays alive.

She gave Conner two thumbs up.

Now, she parked herself at the back of the barn, out of site of the cameras, watching the scene through a partially open door in the back of the barn.

If anything happened, she could get inside, put it out with her fire extinguisher.

"Ready with special effects?" Indigo raised her voice at the front of the barn. Through the open door, and the space, Emily watched her raise her hand, ready to call for quiet. She liked Indigo. With her dark hair and golden-brown eyes, she could command the set with a look, as if she knew exactly what she was doing.

Emily drew in a breath. She nodded, even though Indigo wasn't talking to her.

"Roll camera."

A beat. "Roll sound."

Indigo looked at Cosmos, then, "Action."

The eruption of the fire drums reverberated through the entire barn, shaking it, and the flames erupted with a whoosh, blazing up and out of the front doors.

"He's in there! My son is in there!" Blossom ran toward the barn.

Hawken grabbed her around the waist and pulled her back. "I got him! I got him!"

He then launched himself at the fire, flinging open the doors.

The oxygen turned the fire to an inferno, and he flung up his hands, fell back.

Suddenly a stuntman ran straight into the fire. The two fire barrels spat out black smoke, and he covered his face, picked up the dummy off the floor inside the barn, clad in all green, then threw the dummy over his shoulder and rushed back out.

The front doors closed, and just like that, the scene was over.

Now, the fire cannons were supposed to die, but even through the smoke, she could see that the fire still blazed. Sparks fell, the upper levels of straw igniting, falling to earth like the spray of a volcano.

"Turn it off, Swen!" she shouted, and glanced behind her. Swen held the radio switch, depressing it —

The blaze had caught on some of the wooden stalls.

Her turn. "Houston and Dakota—watch for spots. Charlie, the hose!"

She glanced back, and Charlie held the hose while Orion ran for the truck.

A nearby stack of straw sizzled, drying fast under the flames. The place wasn't an inferno, but give it a few minutes.

"I'm going in!" She slid through the door, not wanting to add any more oxygen to the barn. Smoke roiled against the ceiling, and she pulled up her handkerchief even as she sprayed the foam over the fire, stamping it out in spots. Then she hit the stable walls and pointed the container at the ceiling.

The flames sizzled and died under her onslaught, but even as she found more sparks and doused them, the flames from the barrels grew, licking the eaves. More sparks fell.

Get out.

The thought pulsed inside her as her canister died, the last of the foam spraying out. She grabbed her Pulaski and dragged some straw, now on fire, into the dirt and stomped it out. *C'mon, Swen!* Certainly, the propane tank would have run out of fuel by now.

Outside, shouts lifted, and she looked up to see the hay now catching, flames creeping across the ceiling.

Get. Out!

Yes. She turned and headed for the door in the back. Except, just as she turned, sparks from the ceiling, where the fire had crawled across the beam, fell. Ignited the hay bales by the door.

It whooshed into flames.

She skidded to a stop, fell back into the dirt. Flames licked out, igniting more straw—the place would be an inferno in seconds.

Get. *Out!*

Sound mind. Give me a sound mind!

She turned and looked at the barrels, still spitting out fire. They sat ten feet from each other, a wide enough corridor to the door, if they weren't overflowing with fire.

Except, they stood at least three feet tall.

She could go under them, out the front doors.

Emily hit her knees, began to army crawl, her Pulaski in front of her, her helmet over her head, flames dropping around her.

And then, suddenly, the door opened, and a form appeared through the darkness, a man dressed in fire-retardant stunt gear. He dropped to his knees in front of her.

She looked up.

Spenser?

He wore a hood over his head and goggles, but she'd recognize that jawline anywhere.

"Let's get out of here!"

"The fire is too hot! We have to crawl!"

He dropped next to her, his arm over her. "Let's go!"

Wan light spilled in, as the fire was sucked out. But the oxygen had only ignited the entire barn.

It flamed around them.

One of the barrels lurched, fell over.

And then, just like that, they were trapped, Shadrach and Meshach, bombs of straw and hay sparking around them, falling like droplets.

Her shelter. She rolled and grabbed it out of her leg pocket. Stood up.

"What are you doing?"

"Stay down!" Then even as the fire raged around her in a swirl of heat and fury, she shook out the shelter. She stepped on the corners with her feet, held the others with her hands, spread eagle.

Then she fell over him, hitting her knees. "Get your foot in my corner, your hand here, and hold it to the ground!"

The barn floor was dirt, and it was wet, so that helped. Spenser shoved his boot into the bottom corner, put his hand over hers in the upper corner. She let go and grubbed out a hole in the dirt for herself, then for him because he put his arm over her and held down the other corner too. His leg was over hers, and in a second, she realized he'd put himself almost on top of her.

"Put your mouth in the hole and breathe only that air!" She put her head down, face in the hole. Next to her, Spenser did the same.

She started to breathe in. Out. Counting. In for four, out for seven. In for four, out for seven.

And around them, the barn turned into a furnace.

He ran into the inferno without thinking really.

Without any rational thought because — Emily *was in there!*

Spenser had spotted her bright yellow shirt amidst the black smoke, just a wink of it as the fire partially cleared with the efforts of her fire extinguisher.

Then the fire barrels practically detonated, and with them, the impulse to save her.

He wasn't the only one with that reflex — Winchester started running toward the barn a second before it exploded and was jerked off his feet, into the dirt, coughing.

Spenser spotted an extra CarbonX fire-retardant suit before the shoot, and instinct made him grab it and pull it on. He threw up the hood, pulled on goggles and gloves, and even as Cosmos yelled after him, Spenser headed right into the fire.

It wasn't his first go-round with fire, thank you. He'd even done his own stunts after he turned eighteen on *Trek of the Osprey*.

A few had included fire.

Still, the heat swept over him, a sweat breaking down his spine as he cleared the barrels. Ten feet further, he'd spotted her, on the ground.

His plan turned to a fireball as the entire structure ignited. It shook the barn, rained down heated bullets of straw and hay.

Sheesh, he knew this was a bad idea — he'd felt it in his gut all day. He'd been in the business long enough to listen to said gut. He should have said something. But he'd already caused enough trouble with yet another addition to the script.

He grabbed Emily and forced her down, his brain void of options.

Not Emily's, though.

Wow, that was quick thinking with the fire shelter — more like a shiny blanket over the top of them — and there was no way she wasn't turning crispy inside this shake and bake, so he climbed almost over her, helping her hold down the shelter.

"Breathe into the hole!"

Right. The flames roared over him, and he pushed his mouth into the hole that she'd dug.

Breathed.

She was so terribly calm, breathing steadily, and he matched his breaths with the rhythm of her body.

The fire raged around them, the barn in complete chaos, flames washing over them like the sea. The heat seared his back, his legs, his gloves. He closed his eyes.

Breathed.

Shouts rose in the distance but pierced the thunder of the flames. The voices of her team, maybe.

Please, hurry. Don't let the roof fall.

He hiccupped a breath.

"With me, Spense. Breathe."

Right.

Molten droplets fell on the shelter, even as the flames hissed. Sweat bathed him, his entire body sticky and baking in his suit.

Then, water hit the flames, and the heat began to sizzle, rain pattering on their shelter. Something fell with a crash—maybe a wall, and he froze.

Beneath him, she made a tiny sound, maybe a whimper.

"You okay?" he whispered next to her helmet.

"Yeah. Keep breathing. They're fighting the fire."

He probably imagined the whimper.

He shoved his mouth back into the hole, kept breathing the cooler air there— earthy, maybe a little rank.

Then, just like that, the heat lessened. Then lifted.

Water showered over them, a rainstorm of life. More shouts. He made to move, but she grabbed the front of his jumpsuit with her hand and tucked under his body.

"Stay down. The air is still superheated," she rasped.

"I'm not going anywhere." He settled back over her, the fire dying to a hiss around him.

She lifted her head, turned, met his eyes. Solid, so blue. He was just lost in them for a moment.

"Cosmos is going to murder you," she whispered.

"Probably."

"You shouldn't have run in here."

"Ditto."

"It's my job."

"I'm going to ask Cosmos to fire you. Again."

She narrowed her eyes, her mouth tight.

And shoot, he couldn't help it. He just leaned in and kissed her. Something quick and hot, deep and maybe a little possessive, but all in, his mouth tasting, taking, wanting.

Because this moment, right now, right here, felt as real and honest as he'd ever been. Her, in his arms. Well, not exactly in his arms, but connected, her body tangled with his in this pocket where they'd survived.

And maybe she felt it too, the desperation, if not the connection, because she kissed him back. It took a second, but then she was right there, responding, giving, keeping up with him.

Not even remotely like a movie kiss.

He tucked his knee around her hip, wanting to move her closer, to deepen the kiss when —

"Emily!"

A man's voice. She broke away, met Spenser's eyes with what looked like — what, *panic* —? and then she swallowed and— "Uncle Conner! I'm okay! We're okay!"

The shelter peeled off them like a blanket, and she scooted away from Spenser even as he got to his knees.

He looked up to see a man—her boss, he thought, because it was the same man as the first day—pull her up and into his arms.

"Wow, you scared me!" He lifted her from the shelter, put her down a few feet away, then scanned her entire body as Spenser got up.

"Sorry, Commander. I thought I could put it out—"

"You okay?" The commander turned to Spenser then, his face streaked with sweat, black and dirt under his orange helmet. His eyes were red, maybe with smoke, maybe with fury.

"Yeah."

Conner let her go then backed away, breathing hard.

Around them, the fire still burned, water saturating the charred beams of the barn. Spenser spotted a couple men with a fire hose inside the barn, another two on a hose that shot in water from the back. A small army sprayed down the barn with fire retardant. A few of the special effects crew also held canisters.

"You are so fortunate you aren't under a pile of ash right now," the commander said. "As soon as the fire is out, get out of here!" he said to the crew. "We don't need the roof coming down on us."

Then the commander took Emily by the arm and directed her out the front door, past the burned and deformed barrels.

"What...happened?" Emily said as soon as they cleared the building. She shrugged out of his grip, bent over, clutching her knees, coughing.

"The special effects guy couldn't get the propane turned off," the commander said. "It was jammed at the source. We finally disconnected it—but it was nearly run dry by then."

"I thought you were with the Trouble Boys."

"Yes, I was, but they had everything under control, so I decided to double back. Good thing I did. Of course it was super fun seeing you turning to a crisp in there. Don't think I'll put that on the report."

She gave a weak laugh, so maybe that was good.

Spenser had also bent over, taking off his goggles, coughing a little.

"Have you lost your mind?"

Oh, this one was for him. Spenser lifted a hand to Cosmos, who charged toward him as he stood up. "You could have been killed."

"Wow, Spenser, that was really brave." Kathryn came running up, tears streaking down her face. She pulled him into an embrace. "You scared everybody!"

Oh. Huh. She held on a little longer than he'd expected.

Then, she let him go, grabbed his face, and gave him a kiss. Just a peck, but even he blinked at her as she pulled away. "Don't do that again!"

Right.

Emily was watching him.

The air was soggy and hot, the set smelling of campfire. More shouts as the hotshots and crew moved equipment away from the fire.

Winchester sat on the edge of the set, an oxygen

mask to his mouth, the set medic taking his blood pressure.

He unzipped the jumpsuit as Cosmos stood there, still shaking his head. "Who do you think you are, a stuntman?"

"No, I just—I saw her in there—"

"That's not your job!"

"Well maybe it should be! I can ride a horse better than half the stunt guys here. And I can rope, and I can fight, and maybe I'd be better doing stunts than delivering sixteen lines and smiling into the camera!"

"Twenty-four."

A beat.

"Twenty-four."

"Listen. I know you did your own stunts at *Trek*, but this isn't in a studio with wires and mats. You could get seriously hurt. You're not your dad, Spenser. You're an actor, a well-paid one at that, and I'd like to keep you alive all the way to the end of the movie, and maybe even the promotional tour, okay?"

Spenser's jaw tightened.

Cosmos sighed. Looked at Emily. "Are you okay?"

She nodded.

"Good. Then, you," he pointed to Spenser. "And you," Swen, "Come with me."

Spenser wanted to say no. To grab Emily and pull her somewhere safe, away from the chaos and the trouble and the eyes and...

And kiss her again. See if her response was real and not just induced by...well the fact they'd nearly died together.

He looked at her, but she was engaged in her own argument with her boss.

Fine. Later. He caught up to Cosmos and followed him to his trailer.

Cosmos held the door open while Spenser climbed the stairs, followed by Swen.

Then he went inside. Closed the door. Took a long breath and turned. A muscle in his jaw pulsed. If it hadn't been for his words earlier, Spenser might have thought he was getting fired.

"Sit down, gentleman. We have a situation we need to discuss."

Spenser sat on the sofa attached to the wall. Swen folded his arms, standing by the door.

"Every movie set has a few accidents. It's not uncommon to have injuries because of people falling or preparing cables or even getting hurt from some sort of stunt. Ever since the first accident with the house chimney falling, something's not sat right in my gut. And it's not the catering. Then Kathryn's dress caught on fire, and now the barn…something is rotten in the state of Denmark. I had Kathryn's dress sent to a forensic pathologist—there was accelerant on the cloth. And probably on the curtains to the house, the way they went up."

Spenser stared at him, his mouth opening.

"We'll need to investigate what happened today, but I think…" He swallowed, made a face, shook his head. "I think we are being sabotaged."

Swen unfolded his arms. "What? By whom?"

"I don't know." He looked at Swen. "I want you to vet your team."

"I know every single one of them," he said. "We've worked together for years."

"What about props and set design?" said Win.

"Yes, I'll talk to the set designer and ask her about her crew."

"But it could be anyone with the script and opportunity," said Spenser. "A stuntman, sound, a gaffer, even a grip. Or someone we haven't even thought of."

Silence.

Cosmos nodded, then ran a hand behind his neck. "We have a week left of shooting. I don't want to have to take this back to the lot—we'd have to reserve space, and we're so close to the end. We just have the town shots and the final shootout at the Irish ranch house after Kathryn is kidnapped. Just keep your eyes open."

"We have a break in the filming tomorrow. Emily and I can ride out to the house tomorrow and do a safety check on it," Spenser said.

Cosmos' mouth tightened. "Fine. But please, don't do anything...crazy."

"Me?" Spenser grinned, already looking out the window for Emily. "Never."

CHAPTER 8

"Calm down, you're fine."

Emily stared at herself in the mirror. No more soot, her eyes had cleared, and she'd stopped shaking.

See? Just. *Fine.*

Banging on the bathroom door yanked her away from the moment under the fire shelter when the flames swept over them, and she stifled a scream as she breathed into her hole.

"Em! Are you all right?" JoJo's voice.

"Yeah. I'll be right out." See, her voice didn't even shake.

She blew out her breath, grabbed a towel and wiped the moisture from her face, then turned and opened the door. "What's up?"

JoJo and Sanchez stood in the narrow hallway, both of them changed out of their fire uniforms, back into jeans and T-shirts. Sanchez had pulled her black hair back into a tight ponytail. JoJo's was down, still wet from a shower, probably at the fire house.

Emily had gotten into her truck and driven straight back to her house. The last—very last—thing she needed was a debrief with her team.

She knew she'd screwed up, and badly. And it didn't help that Uncle Conner's voice just kept thrumming through her, on repeat.

Fear wins when it makes you do something stupid. That kind of behavior is dangerous—not just for you, but for your crew.

She could have gotten herself—and more importantly—Spenser Storm killed.

"Besides you nearly turning to barbecue? We heard about it at the fire house. Are you all right?" This from Sanchez who stood a little taller than JoJo, slimmer, a take no prisoners aura about her that suggested she had a history. But she never talked about her past, just kept her head down, did her job.

Now, a hint of anger, or maybe fear, flickered in her eyes. "The guys are really freaked out."

"So am I." JoJo grabbed Emily's hand. She tugged, then pulled her into a hug. "I'm so glad you're safe." She held her a second, then pushed her away. "I remember when I had to deploy my fire shelter. I never want to go through that again."

"Yeah, me either."

"Although," said Sanchez, one side of her mouth quirking up. "I did hear that you shared a shelter with Spenser Storm." She raised an eyebrow to go with the quirk of her mouth.

"He tried to rescue me. It was stupid—he could have gotten killed, and it would have been my fault." She shook her head. "Maybe I should resign from the team."

She pushed away from JoJo and headed out to the kitchen. Opened the fridge. She wasn't even a smidgen hungry, so she closed it.

"We're headed out to the Hotline. There's a

country music guy there tonight. Oaken Fox. He's here to do some music video for the movie, apparently, and he's going to shoot part of the video down at the Hotline. Maybe play a couple songs from his new album. Some of the actors are going to be there too. Maybe Winchester Marshall. Or Trace Wilder. Come with us."

Except, that would be exactly where Spenser might head to decompress, and frankly, she simply couldn't face him.

Not after she'd practically attacked him. One second, she'd been whispering to him to stay put, and then next, well, she wasn't exactly sure what happened. Yeah, he started it—she recalled that much. But mostly she remembered closing her eyes and trying not to wreck the dream where Quillen Cleveland was kissing her.

But it was so much bigger than that, too, because it wasn't Quillen who'd rushed in to save her, but Spenser. Although, it was so like his *Trek* character to do something sacrificial and brave and heroic that it *felt* like Quillen.

Talk about living out your wildest fantasy.

Then, of course, she opened her eyes and woke up from the dream and realized she'd grabbed the poor man and held him down and, oh boy.

And then he'd kissed her.

Frankly, now that she thought about it, maybe she'd given off some sort of kiss me, we survived a fire desperate signal, and it had been just a...what? Pity kiss?

No, not that either, because he was definitely enthusiastic.

Oh, she didn't know what—

"Emily?"

She blinked, looked at JoJo. "Um—"

"The Hotline?"

"Oh. No. I think I've had enough excitement for one day."

"You sure you're going to be okay?"

"Mmmhmm. I'll probably just curl up in a blanket and watch something soothing."

"Like what? *When Calls the Heart*?"

She'd been thinking about an old *Trek of the Osprey* rerun, but whatever.

"Maybe we should stay home." JoJo looked at Sanchez.

"Nope. Nope, I'm fine." She headed down the hall. "See, this is me, getting my blanket."

She grabbed the handle of her door.

"Whoops, not *the* blanket!"

She stopped and turned, and JoJo was wide-eyeing her, eyebrows up. "Ixnay on the anketblay."

What?

Then she turned. "Good to see you, Spenser. Yeah, she's here."

Emily stilled. Spenser Storm was *here?*

JoJo turned to her, more wide-eyes. "Um, we were just leaving? Right? Or maybe staying?"

Emily came down the hall. "Leaving." She put her hand on JoJo's shoulder and turned her.

And right there, standing at the door, was Quillen Cleveland, the rescuer, dressed in jeans and flipflops and a T-shirt. His hair windblown, wearing a hint of a real, not made up, five o'clock shadow, concern in those beautiful pale blue eyes.

Or maybe *not* Quillen, because he was painfully,

breathtakingly real the way he stepped in and said, his voice low, "I wanted to check on you."

Behind him, JoJo put her hand to her chest, arm to her forehead, as if to swoon.

Whatever. "They were just leaving."

"Fine. No blankets." JoJo pushed Sanchez out the door. Sanchez looked at her and winked.

What did they think was going to happen here? Because it was one thing to share a relief kiss, and entirely another for Spenser to...well, what was happening, anyway?

This was not a fairy tale where Cinderella ended up with the prince.

Although, shoot, she had some terribly wild hopes.

"How are you?" she said softly, her voice ridiculous. As if she was what, shy?

"I'm still a little freaked out, to be honest." He still stood at the door.

"Um...are you hungry?"

"Yep."

"How about a pizza?"

"I was thinking about Mac and Cheese, but that's fine." He pulled out his cell phone. "I have an account at Backdraft Pizza."

Of course he did. And when he called, he called the woman by name, laughed with her, and said, "Thanks, Darlin'" like he might be a cowboy, too.

And that helped pop the bubble a little because suddenly she was seeing Kathryn Canary kissing him. *Hello.*

See. Clearly the kissing thing was bigger in her head than his.

He hung up. "It'll be here in thirty minutes."

"I can make some lemonade."

"Perfect. Probably better than shots, right?"

She laughed, and the sound was way too high, too strange. Now she wanted to climb under the table. Instead, she fled to the cupboard. "Are you here to tell me I'm fired?"

He shook his head. "I was kidding."

"Maybe you shouldn't have been. I was... impulsive. And it nearly got you killed." Her chest squeezed a little to admit it, but maybe freeing too. "Facing your mistakes, your close call sometimes releases the trauma, lets you talk about it. Trauma debriefing 101. I don't know what I was thinking. I thought we'd covered all our bases—clearly, I am not the right person for this safety gig."

"It's not your fault." He slid onto a high-top chair at the counter. "Don't tell anyone, but Cosmos thinks that maybe we're being sabotaged. Kathryn's gown had accelerant on it, and so did the drapes that caught fire in the house."

She had pulled out a lemonade packet and now turned to look at him. "Really? Wow. Someone trying to shut down the movie?"

"Maybe. Or maybe it's personal."

A beat.

"You?"

"I don't know. I had this crazy fan threaten me after I wouldn't read his script at comic con."

She hid a smile.

"What? The danger is real."

Now she laughed. "Yes. Of course. Sorry." She held up her hand. "I'd volunteer to protect you, but you'd probably end up, I don't know, trapped somewhere, or burning to death."

"Agreed."

"Hey!"

"Just saying. Maybe someone needs to protect *you*."

"And you're volunteering?"

He looked at her. "Maybe."

Oh. *Oh.*

She turned back, shook the lemonade envelope and opened it.

"We don't know who would sabotage the movie. Someone who doesn't want the movie made?" He lifted a shoulder. "We just need to be extra careful this next week as we finish filming. From there, all the scenes are at the movie lot, indoors, and Cosmos will hire extra security."

She nodded.

"Emily?"

A beat, and when she looked up, he was standing beside her.

"What are you — ?"

He touched her face. "I'm not sure if I'm supposed to apologize or maybe…"

She swallowed. "Maybe?"

His hand cupped her jaw, his thumb soft against her cheek. "I didn't ask the first time. But I was wondering if I could kiss you."

Her mouth opened.

A beat.

He took a breath, dropped his hand. "Okay."

"Wait —" Then she turned to him, put her hand on his chest. His heart thundered under her palm. As if he was…Was Spenser Storm *nervous*? "Stop."

He stilled.

"I…am still sort of buzzing from today, and I need to know that you're not just here because, somehow, you feel responsible for me. Or sorry for me, or — "

"Are you serious? Emily, you're the most amazing person I've ever met. If it weren't for you, we'd be... well, dead." He put his hand over hers. "And I'm still buzzing too. And maybe this is my own impulsive decision, but — "

"Yes." She lifted her face, stood on her tiptoes. "Kiss me."

Oh, wow, had she just said —

Yep. Because he leaned down, his mouth half-open, as if hungry, and kissed her.

No, *inhaled* her. His hands cradling her face, angling her mouth to meet his, tasting her, pulling her against him, then, because he was so much taller, picking her up and setting her on the island.

Talk about turning a girl's knees weak.

She was nearly even with him now, and she slid her arms over his shoulders, her fingers in his hair, that silky dark hair.

What was happening here?

Never before had she been kissed like Spenser Storm kissed her, deep and long, like he actually meant it, and frankly she simply lost herself.

The trauma of the day dropped away, and with it, even her fantasy of kissing Quillen Cleveland, because this man — *this man* wasn't Quillen. Sure, he was charming and brave and had risked his life for her, but he was also just a little vulnerable and sweet and...

Shoot, she was in terrible, terrible trouble.

Because Uncle Conner had gotten it right. The man was going to run away, back to Hollywood.

And he would take her heart with him.

Slow down.

Slow. *Down.*

Spenser wasn't exactly sure how he'd gotten from standing in her kitchen asking for a kiss to the rush of desire and longing that seemed nearly insatiable as he pulled Emily closer to him.

Maybe it was the tiny sounds she was making. Or the way she wrapped her arms around his neck, playing with his hair.

Or the sense, even as he did slow them down, that she wasn't allured by his screen persona, but actually, she was kissing him, Spenser Storm.

Which meant, he didn't want to somehow destroy this by becoming someone she'd read about in the tabloids. Liars, all of them. But he wasn't unaware of the reputation his agent had helped ignite, especially during his Tiger Beat years.

And then there was his stint as a model for Abercrombie. So, yeah, he slowly pulled away, touched her forehead with his. "So…"

"So," she said, and smiled.

And maybe God was on his side because his phone chirruped with the delivery driver's text. "Pizza's here."

He left her on the island and practically fled to the door, and when he'd returned, she'd finished making the lemonade. He set the pizza box on the island, and she brought over the pitcher and a couple of plates — and it all suddenly felt very, very awkward.

Oh no.

Then, "For the record, I do know CPR."

He looked at her.

She grinned at him. "You're sort of white, like you might be freaking out, so I thought I'd let you know that I could save your life. If I had to. Again."

"Um, I think we're even." He opened the box, but his heart had restarted, so maybe she had saved him, at least a little.

"What? I was the one who grabbed the fire shelter."

"Please. Ten more seconds and you would have been under the barrel when it exploded."

Her eyes widened then. "Oh."

Uh oh. "I was just—no, no, let's not go back there. Sorry. I was—"

"I'm just playing with you, Storm. Keep your shorts on. What kind of pizza did you get?"

Wow, he liked her. "Pepperoni. Mushroom." He opened the box.

"My favorite." She grabbed a piece and slid it onto a plate. "Comfort food. Best trauma therapy ever." She had poured him a glass of lemonade, and one for herself, and now took hers to the sofa. Sat down. Picked up the remote. "Comfort television, your pick."

He added a piece to his plate. "*Father Murphy* reruns on TV Land."

She pulled up the menu. "Really?"

He sat on the sofa next to her. "My dad was a stuntman on the show—it was his first gig, and he liked watching it with me. Said there weren't too many shows he'd let me watch. It's a great series about a guy who pretends to be a priest to help some orphans. He falls in love with this schoolteacher and in the end, they adopt the orphans."

"That's very sweet."

"It's that or CSI."

"That's a big jump."

"Dad was also a stuntman on that show for three years. In fact, his last gig was a jump from a helicopter. Unfortunately, they were filming in a gulch outside the city, and somehow the chopper caught on some electrical lines. There was a child actor aboard, and Dad grabbed the kid as the chopper went down, and cushioned his fall. It saved the kid's life, but that's how he died. "

"Oh, Spenser."

"Yeah. They still aired the show. I couldn't watch it for years, but then I did, and...I don't know. Sometimes I rewrite the ending where he lives, you know? Walks away, comes home."

He wasn't sure how this had gotten so serious so fast. He put down his pizza. "Sorry."

"No, that's a great therapy technique when we feel like the truth is too hard. I rewrite that moment when I'm staring at the man who would kidnap me, and instead of taking his hand, I just turn and keep running."

She did what? "Why did you take his hand?"

"He said I could trust him. And I believed him." She made a face. "I was six. And I was scared, so... you know."

"That's terrible."

"Yeah, well, in my rewritten ending, I slap his hand away and run and run and end up in my mom's arms. Or I make myself older and fight back. I like that ending."

He just stared at her. "That's brilliant."

"That's therapy."

"Maybe I should have had therapy. Instead, my

grandfather got me into acting, and suddenly, I could pretend I was someone else, all the time."

"Quillen."

"In a way, he sort of saved me. In my head, I'm as brave as Quillen."

She touched his arm. "Or your dad."

Sheesh, now his chest sort of closed up. He nodded.

"I heard Cosmos today accuse you of wanting to be a stuntman."

His jaw tightened. He drew in a breath. "I'll never be my dad. He was... He was my whole world. Brave and strong. A real cowboy. He wasn't interested in being anything but who he was—a stuntman. He'd grown up watching my grandfather go through wives, and girlfriends, and he was just...not that guy. He met my mom at a Billy Graham crusade in Alaska when he was twenty years old. He'd gone there to escape my grandfather, got saved, married my mom, and then decided to come back to Montana when she got pregnant. She had a miscarriage. It took them another ten years before they had me. They moved to Hollywood, and he and mom were both stuntmen and extras until she got pregnant, finally, with me. She died during childbirth."

"Oh, Spenser, I'm so sorry."

"My dad was amazing. He took me everywhere with him. I was often on set. In fact, I was on set the day he died. I was eight, and we had a camper trailer he'd haul around. I wasn't watching, but I'll never forget the AD coming in to take me to the hospital. My grandfather showed up a couple hours later—he was filming in the area. My dad had died."

She'd gone quiet, her hand on his arm.

"I'll never forget my grandfather coming into the waiting room. He gave me a hug, said that Dad was gone, and that there was press waiting outside. Told me to smile and say my dad was the bravest man I knew. It wasn't a lie."

"Smile?"

"Show business. I started acting just a few months later. And since then… I don't know. I was in a couple movies and then became Quillen. But in truth, maybe I don't know who I am."

"I do. You're Spenser Storm. Cowboy. Actor. Pretty good kisser —"

He grinned at that.

"And every bit as brave as your dad. You don't have to be a stuntman to prove that."

A beat.

Oh boy. Now she was inside his soul, taking a good look around.

"I think your dad would be really proud of you. You're an amazing actor, Spenser, and the world is a better place because you brought a great story on screen once a week for ten years."

"Yeah, that's what the world needs — a great story."

"What? Yeah, it does. People need stories. For entertainment. For inspiration. For hope. A great story — a great character — can get inside our hearts and inspire. And that's just as lifesaving as running into a fire."

He gave her a look.

She put down her pizza. Stood up. Faced him.

And then, "We go into the stars not because we crave adventure, but we crave something more — the touch of honor. We go to save a hundred lost souls, never mind one of them is my father. We go because every life matters, and every soul is worth the search, worth finding. So, Commander Tarkon, are you with me?"

He blinked at her. "You memorized the speech from season three?"

"Episode four, when they decide to go into the black hole that would fling them across four galaxies. Yes. I was in *tears*."

Oh.

"It sort of reminded me of—and I know this sounds weird—of Jesus going after the lost sheep. And somewhere deep inside, I was that lost sheep, needing to be found."

He saw her then, just for a moment, a child, lost in the dark.

And now she wiped her cheek. "So don't you dare say that you're not a hero. Because to a teenager who was still trying to figure out if God cared, the story of Quillen's quest to find his father very much mattered."

Sheesh, now he might cry. "Okay."

"Okay. Now eat your pizza." She picked up hers then sat back on the sofa.

But again, she'd sort of saved him because the terrible tightness in his chest released. He picked up his pizza. Then he reached for the remote. "We might be able to find a rerun of *Trek of the Osprey*."

She took it away from him.

"I would rather sit here with the real Quillen Cleveland and finish off this pizza."

He glanced at her. She was smiling, wagging her eyebrows.

"If you want, we could run lines. I read the script. You get the girl."

Oh wow, he desperately hoped so.

Still. "Actually, that's the thing. I still think it doesn't work."

"Really? I love this movie."

"Except in the end, Winchester dies at the hands of Irish, and yeah, I get the girl, but… I don't know. It's not the ending in the book."

"Which is…"

"Both men die."

"Hmm." She took a sip of her lemonade. "Not very inspiring."

He stared at her. "That's it. The ending is…not inspiring. Happy, but not…inspiring."

"So, what are you going to do about it?"

"There is nothing I can do. The story isn't mine."

She drew up her legs, crossed them. "But if you could, how would you end it?"

He considered her, sitting there in the pool of light from the lamp, dressed in a T-shirt, her hair still wet from a shower, her green-blue eyes pinned to his. And for a second, her words simply landed, found soil.

I would rather sit here with the real Quillen Cleveland and finish off this pizza.

This. This was how he'd end it. With a woman who saw *him*, not Cleveland, or even the guy who'd run in to save the day, but the guy who just wanted to get it right.

The thought caught him up, wrapped around him, held him.

Slow down. Just slow down…

Not a hope.

CHAPTER 9

"Try not to kill me!"

Emily tightened her hold around Spenser's waist, her voice lifting over the motor of the Polaris ATV as Spenser drove over the dry, rutted land—a shortcut to the old White homestead, where the final shoot would take place.

Such gorgeous country, with the mountains rising around them, the sun high in the clear blue sky. Here, the air smelled of pine and balsam, the land ablaze with pink bitterroot and tiny blue forget-me-nots that swayed in the breeze.

They drove along a bumpy dirt path, through a gulch, a tumble of granite and rock rising on one side, dotted with scrub brush and scruffy pine. On the other side, the gulch dropped to green pasture, before dropping again to the cool, fast running Kootenai river to the east.

Around them, mountains touched the clouds, the land brutal and unforgiving.

"Just hang onto me!"

Oh, she was hanging on. She had her hand

gripped around his washboard waist, her legs pressed against his thighs.

Still, she hadn't hated Spenser's grand idea that they run a general safety check on the location when she'd arrived on set this morning. Apparently, he had the day off from shooting.

A day that he spent the first few minutes pulling her behind the production trailer, his hands braced on either side of her shoulders, trapping her so he could kiss her.

Oh, he was sunshine to her soul. Something about him just made her feel...wanted.

Or at least not lost.

"You're going to get me fired," she'd said, the taste of coffee on her lips. Oh, he was breathtaking today in a *Drifters* T-shirt, that might be just a little too small for him, and a pair of faded jeans, cowboy boots. He even wore a black Stetson, and it fit him so well, it probably wasn't a prop.

"Trust me."

She drew in a breath. Trying. But she didn't say that because, well, she didn't want to be that girl who said...what happens next?

But it hung in her mind last night after he'd left. After they'd finished eating, then watched an episode of Law and Order—except not really because most of it they'd ended up kissing.

And Spenser Storm could kiss.

Please, let it be real.

Although, if it was a fairy tale, she intended to squeeze every last moment from it, starting with spending the day with Spenser on the ATV, driving around the Montana foothills.

Swoon.

He'd grabbed a couple sandwiches from craft services, along with bottled water, and she put them into her backpack, with her phone and an extra charger, just in case. She also added sunscreen and a handkerchief to hold her hair back.

"According to the drawing, the big ambush scene is supposed to take place just beyond this mountain." Emily held the surveyor's map of Old Henry's land in her hand.

They'd traveled maybe a mile, or less, across country, between towering balsam and lodgepole pine, following the gulch as it turned east under the shadow of the Kootenai mountains.

The map slapped against her, folding over itself in the wind, and he slowed as she plastered it against his back.

"Okay, so, the house is set back from the road a ways. I think we follow the gulch and just past this mountain, we'll run right into it."

He had stopped to survey the land, however. "Just gorgeous. So much different than lowlands where the Flying S sits. There, the mountains are just a blue line in the distance."

"I snagged this map from the fire office," she said. "If you keep following this gulch to the west, you'll run into the old house where they're supposed to film, and then beyond that, the valley where there's a resort with an airstrip and a horse farm. There's a kids' wildfire camp to the north of that, but all this land," she opened her hand and spread it over the map, "is owned by the White family. It's a massive piece, about thirty miles of acreage along the river, and into the valley. And, there's a huge gold and silver mine on it.

Apparently, that's how the Whites made all their money."

"Are you talking Isaac White, the president?"

"I think so. I'm not sure, but I know he owns land in Montana, so…" She lifted her shoulder. "I did some Googling. The ghost town you're filming at started in 1870 after a silver strike in the mine, and it served the mining community—saloon, bank, trading post, livery. A school and a church. Over two thousand people lived in the area, including the mining company. Nearer the mine, there are some cabins and an office. Who knows if they're still standing, though. The mine is huge, however. There's supposedly a north entrance, too, and tunnels that run for miles. According to the map, it even connects to an underground cave system. The entrance should be around here, somewhere in that mountainside." She pointed to the rise in the land ahead, a mix of towering pine and sharp-edged granite.

"Apparently, the town was decimated in 1889 after diphtheria hit it. The mine shut down in 1912, and the town died over the next decade. It was eventually acquired by the Whites. I think they use it for hunting trips now."

"I saw some moose tracks earlier. Ready?"

For what? Probably not. "Yes."

"Hang on." The four-wheeler lurched. Sputtered. "Just a second." He depressed the ignition.

She took a moment to admire his forearms, the nice tan he was getting.

Stop.

The four-wheeler kicked on, and he cut them east, the dirt path rutted and littered with rock. They slowed as they traversed a stream, a runoff to the massive river.

They rounded the mountainside. "There's the mine." The land flattened and spread out into a grassy tarmac. An old building, the faded wooden walls partially standing, the roof fallen to the center, listed to one side near a timber-braced rocky maw.

He slowed and then worked his way off the path toward the mine entrance. Closer, it seemed the river ran from it, just a swampy trickle, but moisture that bled from the rocky entrance. Braces framed the top and sides of the entrance, and more timber ran into the tunnel. A rusty pipe, probably for ventilation, ran along the ceiling, along with a black cable for electricity.

"Want to go in?"

"No, thanks. It looks spooky."

"Whooo," he said, sounding like a ghost.

She whacked his shoulder, then pointed to a cabin, still intact, farther down the gulch. "Let's check that out."

The four-wheeler sputtered again, but he restarted it and motored them along the bumpy swath of land toward the cabin, maybe two hundred yards away.

The cabin wasn't huge—peeled logs stacked on top of each other, with pitch between the cracks, and a wooden roof. But as they drew closer— "Is that smoke coming out of a stovepipe?" She pointed.

He slowed the ATV. "I think so."

The cabin sat on a small hill, cluttered with pine trees and scrub, and as they drew around the curve of the land, shouts lifted.

He slowed.

Then a shot rang out, fracturing the air. Birds

scattered. More shouts and two more shots. And from the front of the cabin, burst a man. Long hair, tied back, he wore a black shirt, jeans, and a baseball hat.

He turned, shot back into the house, just as another man stumbled out after him. Rail thin, dark hair, he also held a gun and now turned and fired back at the house.

"Spenser—"

He was already gunning the ATV. But of course, it sputtered again, died.

Ponytail Gunman spotted them. "Hey!"

"Spenser!"

He was turning over the motor, but the engine just whined.

Skinny had mounted a dirt bike.

"Spense—"

"C'mon!" He hopped off the four-wheeler, grabbed her hand, and pulled her off.

The driver with his bike skittered down the rocky hillside.

"Run!" Spenser had her hand, pulling her along the path, heading toward the trees.

A shot, and a bullet winged past them, and he ducked, kept running.

Another shot, and she glanced behind to see the biker had hit the road.

Spenser shoved her off toward the forest, sparse as it was, as another bullet pinged past them.

"Run, Em!"

The bike's motor burned the air, louder behind them. They reached the collapsed structure, and he pulled them behind it. More shots.

"The mine!"

No, no—but now the second man had cleared the hill, roaring toward them.

The cabin exploded. A massive thunder of timber and stone and fire that blazed over the tree line. Flames licked the air, edged in black, ferocious and deafening.

The bikers spurted out of the black cloud, gunning for them.

Spenser gripped her hand and took off, running hard for the mine opening. He splashed into the water, dragged her in, and ran straight into the dark maw.

More shots pinged against the walls even as they sloshed deeper into the mine, the light blinking out too fast.

"Spenser—"

"Don't let go!" He kept pulling her into the darkness. Shouts at the entrance echoed down the chamber.

She tripped, and he caught her, then kept going deeper. The darkness thickened, just a hint of gray now. "What if we fall into a pit, or a shaft?"

"Good point." He stopped then, turned and pulled her against him, his arms around her, backing up until they pressed against a wall. "Shh."

Shouts, more shots, and she closed her eyes, her focus on his arms around her, the hard planes of his warm body, his thundering heartbeat.

Swearing sounded, but it seemed to be farther away.

"We need to get out of here, so we can call my hotshot team, tell them about the fire before it gets out of control. It's so dry out—it could turn into a wild—"

A terrible thunder erupted, careening through the tunnel. Shook the earth, and dirt showered them.

What little light remained snuffed out.

A beat, and the cacophony stilled, leaving only the explosions of her heartbeat.

"Did they—did they blow up the entrance?" She whispered, but the cave seemed to swallow her words.

Then everything inside her shattered when he drew in a breath and said, in a shaky whisper. "I think we're trapped."

"Maybe this wasn't such a brilliant idea." Spenser stepped back, his fingers raw. Sweat saturated his body despite the dank chill that permeated the mine. "I don't know how thick this cave-in is, but we're not moving these rocks."

Emily stood behind him, her cell phone flashlight aimed to the clutter of rock and timber that had exploded to block the entrance to the mine. Thick chunks of granite, wood, and boulders clogged the entrance.

"We're lucky the entire thing didn't come down on us." She shone her light along the broken beams that still clung to the ceiling. "I'm not so sure we should even try and move this debris. Feels like it's keeping the whole thing from caving in more."

Wow, she was brave. Sure, she'd screamed when the mine entrance collapsed, had hung onto him, trembling, her face in his chest.

But it only kept him from doing the same actually, and instead, he took a deep breath, held her tight.

Don't panic. He wasn't sure who said it first, but it

became a sort of mantra as the dust settled, as he found his cell phone in his pants pocket and turned on the flashlight.

"Don't panic." He'd held out his hand, and she took it.

"Don't panic," she said as they picked their way to the front of the mine.

"Don't panic," he whispered as they stared at their only way out.

Now, she flicked off her flashlight—his was still lighting the cave, his cell phone propped up on some rocks—and came up to him, wrapped her arms around his waist. "Don't panic."

"I think I'm way beyond panic." He embraced her, pressing a kiss to her dusty hair.

"At least we're not shot at."

"Right. What do you think that was?"

"I dunno. Meth lab? That's more likely than something rigged to blow on purpose."

He looked down at her. Dust streaked her face, layered her hair, her eyes so blue in his. "Really? Out here?"

"Oh, you'd be surprised. It's not unusual for hotshots to walk into a field of marijuana or some drug camp while we're out fighting fires. Or at least that's what my roommate JoJo says."

"No wonder the place blew up." He scratched at the stubble on his jaw. "Pretty careless, no matter what their beef was with each other that led to a gunfight." And then they'd shot at him and Emily.

She let him go and nodded, her face grim. "Maybe one of the shots hit something explosive." Her hands on her hips, she faced the darkness ahead of them.

"So, now what? This mine is layers deep, with tunnels in all directions."

"There are rails here. Maybe they lead to another exit. Let's see that map."

She'd pulled off her backpack and now retrieved it, pulling out the map from inside. He fetched his phone and shined the light on it.

"It only marks the entrances. Here, where we came in, and then there are some cabins up this way, about a half-mile away. There's a house over here to the west, but I'm not sure it's connected to the mine."

"What's this?" He pointed to a line on the eastern edge of the map.

"That's the Kootenai river."

"We followed that for a while coming up."

"Yeah, it's probably a half mile from us."

"Does it connect to the mine?"

"I don't know."

"What about the cave system you mentioned?"

"That's connected somehow to the mine, but I have no idea where, or how."

He stood up and shone his light down the shaft.

"Okay," she said. "My dad is a caver, and he always says the best thing to do is follow a pattern. So, we go down the shaft, and every time it turns, we go left. And take a picture of where we're going. We keep track of how many times we turn, so if we have to go right, we note it. And let's turn down the beam on your light, conserve energy."

He turned the light down, let go of a couple breaths. Looked up at her.

She held onto the wall of the cave, her eyes closed.

"What are you doing?"

"Praying."

He wrapped his arms around her, held her to himself. "I haven't been much of a person of faith since Coco the Great died, but…she used to pray *The Lord is my rock, my fortress and my deliverer.*"

"Fear or Faith."

"What?"

"Something Conner said to me. Am I going to live in fear or faith?"

"I don't think we have much choice right now."

She turned, slid her hand into his. "Maybe that's the answer. Is there ever really a good choice?"

Then she stared down the tunnel, into the darkness. A rusty metal pipe ran across the top, a black wire affixed to the wall, the rock clearly chipped out in places, possibly dynamited in other places.

Faith was the only real answer.

The temperature fell as they walked deeper, the tracks veering away, the path taking them down a staircase, then to another level.

The tracks split as they came to a larger chamber.

"Left?" she said.

He picked up a couple rocks and set them together on the tracks, another one making a T. "Just in case we come back this way." Then he took a shot of the entrance behind him and followed her into the darkness.

The tunnel grew smaller, just the size of a train cart, maybe, and he had to duck then crouch. "I don't love this."

She was on her hands and knees now. "It feels strange that miners would crawl through this space."

"Maybe this is for the track. Let's double back."

He turned around, and they followed the tracks out, hitting another expansive chamber.

"Where's our marker?" This chamber connected to two more, with stairs descending to more depths. The train track ran to a tunnel ahead, again tight, with a larger tunnel to the right.

"Where's our original tunnel?" Emily said.

He pulled up his picture. "I don't know. Did we miss a turn?"

She closed her eyes. "Okay, take a picture." She set up another marker, pointing back to the tunnel they'd emerged from.

Water clung to the walls, the mine seeping minerals, the smell of rust and dirt thick in the darkness. He flashed his light down the larger tunnel and led the way, her hand in his. His light fell upon the rusty piping. "I think we need to stay in the tunnels where there is piping—the other ones might just be for hauling out ore."

Some forty feet down the tunnel, his light fell upon a caged electrical panel. On a chance, he threw the breaker.

Nothing.

"Wait—Spense, do you feel that?"

He stilled. Nothing but her hand in his, the sense of doom hovering nearby. "No. What?"

"Air, I thought. Fresh air. Maybe I imagined it."

"Which direction?"

"In front of us."

He continued to grip her hand and headed into the darkness. They came to another stairway, down, no sign of the rails. A smaller corridor led to the right.

"Down?"

She closed her eyes. "I don't know. I don't feel it anymore."

"I don't want to go down." He showed his light into the corridor. Narrow and dark, it raised the small hairs on his neck.

"I think down is the only way," she whispered.

The uneven risers were cobbled together by rotted wood. He shone his light down. "I can't see the end."

She turned, looked back where they came. "Spenser, there are two tunnels behind us."

He turned. Stilled. "We did it again."

"Mmmhmm."

Blowing out a breath. "Okay. Down we go." He glanced at her in the wan light.

She gave him a smile. "C'mon Quillen, into the darkness, into the adventure."

"Seriously." But he turned to the stairs. "Please let this thing not crumble on us." A metal railing was affixed to the rock, and he tested each step as they descended, the wood creaking, cracking, flexing under their weight. Unlit lanterns hung from the walls.

He looked back, and only her face was illuminated above him.

Yeah, this was a bad idea.

Especially when the board snapped beneath his step. He lurched forward, hit the next board and it, too, cracked.

"Spense!"

He felt her hand on him a second before the world dropped beneath him. Suddenly, he was falling into darkness, a scream echoing off the unforgiving granite walls.

CHAPTER 10

AND JUST LIKE THAT, EVERY NIGHTMARE CAME true.

Her scream bounced against the walls, the metal railing, the stairs, and right into the core of her soul as he ripped away from her grip.

"Spenser!"

His cell phone fell, the light winking out into the darkness.

No—no—

And then he landed. Not miles away, thankfully, but closer because his grunt lifted, followed by a deep moan and then terrible, short breaths.

His phone hit the dirt face down, just the slightest glow emanating, but in the pitch darkness, it seemed like the light of a thousand suns. She barely made him out moving some ten feet below.

"Hang on! I'm on my way!"

She pulled out her phone from her pants pocket and now turned on the flashlight.

He'd fallen yes, less than ten feet, and lay at the bottom of the stairs, most of the rungs broken, so that had to hurt. He held his arm to himself.

She pulled out her handkerchief and tied it to her head. Then shoved the phone into it like a headlamp. Gripping the railing, she worked her way down on the risers of the steps.

He had sat up, his eyes closed when she reached him, still holding his arm. "Is it broken?"

"No, it's dislocated. I'll be okay. Just help me up."

She reached around his waist as he pressed up against the wall.

He bent over, his injured arm hanging down.

"What are you doing?"

"My dad's trick." He tucked his fingers under his foot. Then, he slowly pulled up, keeping his fingers tucked under. The shoulder strained, then suddenly popped into place.

"That worked."

"Yep." He slid back down to the ground. "I'll need a sling."

She took off her handkerchief, then looped it under his arm and tied it behind his head. He blew out his breath. "Okay, that's better."

And then she spotted the blood, coming from his thigh. "Spense, you're bleeding!"

"Yeah, I nicked it on the way down."

She shone her light on it. The gash was easily six inches long, maybe a half-inch deep.

"That's not a nick—it's deep. You need stitches."

"It's fine."

She looked at him. And then, shoot, it all rushed over her. No, no—

But the horror of it simply bubbled up. She put a hand to her mouth, but the whimper came anyway.

Stop. *Stop.*

The whimpering turned to a shuddering breath, and her eyes filled.

"Emily?"

She held up her hand. "I'm fine—"

"You're *not* fine." He put his hand to her cheek. "Em. We're okay, we're okay—"

"We're not okay, Spenser! We're lost in a cave, and you're hurt—and you could even have internal bleeding, and we have no idea where we are and... and it's too hard."

He stared at her. "What's too hard?"

"Faith! Faith is too hard! It's just...one minute you're fine and everything is beautiful and the next you're shot at. Or...falling down stairs or...

"Or in a train wreck?"

"Yeah. In a train wreck. Or...how about your dad is dying right in front of you...or you're trusting the wrong thing and suddenly the stairs disintegrate under you and... It's just *too hard*." She wiped her cheeks, but the tears burned her eyes. "I'm tired of fighting all the time. Tired of being brave and trying to keep the screams inside. But I'm not brave, Spense." She looked at him. "I'm not brave. I'm scared. Most of the time, that...something terrible is going to happen again."

"I know." He went quiet beside her. And when he spoke again, his voice turned soft, gentle. "That's why you do things like run into a burning building—"

"But I can't stop it! Even then—it blows up in front of me, and I'm just making it worse."

He looked at her, and what did she expect of him? He was no more in control of the situation than she was.

"I think maybe that's the point," he said softly.

"What?"

"When we try and control things, we only make them worse."

He looked away now, his mouth a tight line. "We think we know how to solve the problem, how to fix our broken pieces, but we haven't a clue, so we do stupid things and pretend to be people we're not, trying to find something that makes us feel less panicked."

She stared at him. "Like model underwear?"

He took a breath. "Like ten years of playing a character you desperately want to be like, only to have it end. And then you discover that you're not him. And never will be. So then you go model underwear."

Oh.

"I don't think I want to be an actor anymore."

She blinked at him. "What?"

He turned to her. "I don't know. Maybe I do. I was Quillen for so long, I sort of lost myself. Or maybe I just grew up with him as my mask, and then when it was over, I didn't know who I was. Maybe I still don't."

She sat beside him, her back to the wall. "Me either. I don't want to be a hotshot. I just want my dad to want me on his team. And I want my mom to think I'm as smart as she is. And even if my dad did want me on his team, I think...I think maybe Uncle Conner is right. There's something else out there for me. I just can't get my fingers around it."

His hand wove into hers, and he simply sat in the darkness and held it. The warmth reached through her, into her bones, her cells.

"Conner said that when we live in trauma and in

fear, we live outside the presence of God. And that's when we make bad decisions."

He looked at her. "Maybe it's not about where you are, or what's happening around you, but who you're with. The presence of Jesus, the Prince of Peace. Maybe that's what makes your soul well."

She stared at him.

"Coco the Great used to tell this story about her adopted mom. She was a wing walker."

"Like on an airplane?"

"Yes. And her husband was a pilot. She said that he would do aerials, full circles in the sky, and that at some point, the airplane would stop flying, and just start falling. Eventually, it would reach an angle where the wind caught it and saved them. Maybe that's what it means to be well—to know you're safe, even when you feel like you're falling."

"Or you're lost?"

He looked at her. "Or hurt. Or in a fire."

"Or at the bottom of the earth." She reached out and retrieved his phone. "Your screen is broken."

He turned the phone off, shoved it into his pocket.

Then he turned back to her. And before she could say anything, he put his hand around her neck, pulled her to himself and kissed her.

Oh. What?

But she grabbed onto the collar of his shirt and held them there. Braced her hand on the rock above his hurt shoulder and kissed him back. Just a moment of hope, perhaps, but enough that when he let her go, he took a breath. Nodded.

"What was that?"

"Inspiration." He pushed up the wall, groaning on

his way. "And a distraction from how much my shoulder hurts."

She got up beside him, held out her phone. Ahead of them, two tunnels wove into the darkness. "Which way?"

He took her hand. "Which way, Jesus?"

She smiled. Okay. She'd bite. "Which way, Jesus?" And that's when she felt it again. "Wind."

He looked at her. And a smile lifted. "Wind."

She looped his arm around her shoulders. "Let's get out of here."

They took off down the tunnel. Drips sounded, plinks in the darkness. They came to the end of the tunnel, found a branch and —

"Water."

"I hear it too."

She directed them to the right. "There's no more electricity or ventilation tubes here." In fact, the walls seemed less etched, more natural, scraped out. "I think we've connected to the cave."

The rushing sounded louder, the walls became wetter, and then...light. It pressed against the far wall, in a turn ahead, cascading down the shaft, fading as it reached them, but — *light.*

He picked up his pace, even with the occasional grunt, and turned the corner.

Gorgeous. A deep turquoise lake, clear to the bottom, spread out in a massive chamber. Above, tiny pinpricks of light cast onto the surface.

At one end, the lake bubbled over rocks, then fell into shadow, and beyond that the loud chatter of a waterfall.

"Perfect. Now all we need is a barrel." Spenser reached for a nearby boulder and sat down.

"It has to lead out, right? Maybe to the river?"

The lake appeared about fifty feet long, maybe thirty feet wide. She went to the edge. It seemed shallow, but when she threw a rock in, it sank for a while. "It's deep."

Blood had saturated his pants leg, dripping off his cuff.

No way could he swim out, over the falls—which dropped how far?

"We did an on location shoot once for *Trek of the Osprey*," he said. "It was an episode where we were trapped inside a planet—"

"I remember that one. There were these reptiles that glowed in the dark."

"Yeah. We used them to find our way to the surface. But I remember the director had us shooting in a real cave. We had a safety guide there, and he said that if we were ever lost in a cave to follow the sound of water."

She came back over, pulled off her backpack. "Clearly he was never trapped in an underground lake."

"What are you doing?"

"I'm eating a sandwich. Want one?"

"I forgot about the sandwiches! Yes. With everything inside me."

She handed him one.

"This is really good."

And something inside her simply unknotted. He sat there, eating his sandwich, bruised, dirty, bloodied—and still, probably the most handsome man she'd ever met—and she just wanted to cry all over again.

What was Quillen—no, what was Spenser Storm doing with *her*? Kissing *her*?

And maybe she shouldn't ask that. Maybe it didn't matter. Because he didn't seem to act like it mattered.

Maybe, in fact, all of this *was* real.

"Emily?"

"Sorry. I was just really hungry." She smiled at him. "I'll only eat half—keep the other half here with you. Until I get back..." Except, how would she find her way back here?

"Until you get...back?"

"Yes." She sighed. "I'm going for a swim."

"*We're* going for a swim."

She packaged up the other half of her sandwich. "Your shoulder isn't strong enough, and you're still bleeding. I'm the one who can go, so I'm going."

"Over my dead body."

"That's what I'm trying to prevent." She handed him a bottle of water. "Listen. I'm not trying to be brave. I'm doing what has to be done. Someone has to go into the darkness and figure out how to bring us home."

"Oh please, no more Quillen quotes."

"You were the one who brought up *Trek*."

"How big of a fan are you?"

Oh. "One of three billion."

He laughed. Then suddenly, "That's it."

She raised an eyebrow.

"The ending of the movie. I've figured it out. The wrong man gets the girl."

Now? He was rewriting the movie *now*? "*You* get the girl."

"Because Deacon is the only logical choice to make the sacrifice. Because he's already heroic. But that's not a *real* hero. The real hero is the one who is scared and overwhelmed and yet faces the end with courage, because it's the right thing. *Hawken* has to die."

And with that, he got up.

"What are you doing?" She stood up. "Spenser?"

He'd walked to the edge of the lake. She froze as he turned and took off his sling. Winked. "Wait here."

And then, he dove into the water.

Yes, it was impulsive and probably stupid, but something had simply clicked when he'd mentioned the reptiles, and then she said the Quillen quote and what choice did he have?

Let her jump in, get swept away by the current, go over the falls?

That was a big N.O.

So, call him crazy, but he went first.

But it wasn't without forethought. He'd been listening to the water rush—not thunderous with deep gulps plummeting thousands of feet, but a slight rush, as if the falls might be short, the water dump light.

He'd also been staring at the gullet where the water vanished. It seemed that the light casting down from above couldn't be enough to light the chamber, so it had to come from another source. Light bounced off the space above the waterfall, cast into the depths of the lake, so that it was nearly transparent.

Which meant the water didn't plummet into a cave deep below, but outside.

To freedom.

The water slicked away the heat from his shoulder, burned his leg. What he hadn't accounted for was the current. It slammed him against the rocks, and he just barely got a handhold, a foothold before the current pulled him over into the abyss. He came up, gulping breaths, to hear Emily shouting.

"Have you lost your mind?"

"Hold, please!"

He leaned over, into the open space where the falls fell. Please, let there not be rocks below—

The water dropped to a pool some twenty feet below, spraying like a faucet into the late afternoon.

The splash obscured any rocks, so he couldn't be sure if it was clear.

He pulled himself away from the edge, still holding on. Looked back.

She'd vanished.

"Emily!"

He spotted her then, in the water, swimming hard for him.

No, no, because the current—yep, it caught her, and she fought it, kicking for the edge.

He held out his hand. "Grab on!"

She met his grasp, and he couldn't stifle the moan as his shoulder screamed. But he held on, and she got her foot onto the edge and then her other hand and pulled herself up and over him. Breathing hard.

"What were you thinking? I was coming back!"

She stared at him. "Maybe someone should inform me of the Grand Plan before someone dives into the scary lake of death!"

He blinked at her. Grinned.

"So, do we need a barrel?" She didn't smile, just glared at him.

"No. It's not a far drop. And then we're in the river."

"Perfect. And this couldn't have waited until after we finished our sandwiches?"

Oh, he wanted to kiss her again. And just staring at her, fighting a grin, her hair wet and stringy, those green-blue eyes holding his, his heart just about exploded.

He loved this woman. And sure, it might be fast and crazy, but most on-set romances were exactly that way, but he'd never felt anything so powerful, so *right* in all his life.

"What?" She frowned at him. "You okay? How's your shoulder?"

"It's fine." Sheesh. He was turning into a pansy. He reached for her hand. "Together?"

"We're jumping?"

"Falling might be more specific."

"How far?"

"Twenty feet."

"Don't let go."

"Nope. Ready?"

She nodded, took a breath, and suddenly they were in the water, and flying into the open space.

He kept hold of her hand, windmilled his arm, and they splashed down into the pool below.

They sank, slowed, but his feet hit bottom and he pushed up.

Air. Light. He gulped both as he shook the water away. She floated next to him, kicking them away from the churning pool of water.

Twenty feet away, upstream, a higher, thunderous waterfall plunged from a cliff fifty feet high, into the deeper wells of the Kootenai river, so there must be an offshoot that ran through the cave.

The river current had grabbed them, pulled them into the rapids.

"Let go! I can swim!" She shook free of his hand. "Get to the shore!"

The rapids had fingers, grabbing them, stirring them into the rush. Rocks protruded and he pushed off one, spun, spotted her in the froth.

The shore seemed a thousand miles away, a rutted and slick canyon wall.

"Put your feet out!" she shouted. "Feet first down the river!" She slipped past him, on her back, treading water.

He rolled over too, rode the rapids behind her.

She kicked away from rocks, swimming toward the shoreline as the cliffs fell toward flatter land.

The river widened, too, becoming shallower. He kept his head up, managed not to swallow more than a gallon of water, and followed her.

She finally caught herself on a massive boulder that spanned half the river, reached out and he caught her hand. Fighting the current, he managed to grab the boulder, to hoist himself on it.

They lay together, like trout, gasping for air.

The sun had fallen, deep shadows over the river, casting down from the fir-lined mountains that rose around them.

"Do you smell that?" Emily asked.

"Life? Freedom? The sweet smell of anything but a cave?"

"Smoke." She sat up. "Maybe I'm imagining it."

"You're a hotshot. You have fire on the brain."

She laughed, rolled over, and pushed herself up,

looking upstream from where they came. "Maybe I just have…" Her mouth opened.

He was just getting to his feet and now turned.

An ever so thin glow of orange crackled along the tree line to the west.

"We gotta go." They were too late to call in the explosion. "There's already a forest fire."

He followed her across the boulder, and then as she hopped on the other boulders to the shore. "I'll bet it's from the cabin explosion."

"We have no idea where we are, Emily."

"Yes, we do. The river runs southwest. The set is in the direction of the river, and the fire is north. For now. The wind is pushing it south, right toward the movie set."

They reached the rocky shoreline. "We'll keep the sun to our right, then cut west, and we'll hit the dirt path. C'mon." She started down the shore.

"Can we outrun this thing?" He took off after her.

"Fires can move about twenty miles per hour, but the wind isn't high, and there isn't a ton of fuel between the cabin and the set. We'll stay along the river until the sun sets. Then we'll put the moon at our back."

"You sound like you live in the forest."

"My dad was a Green Beret, what can I say?" She had picked up her speed. "He took me orienteering when I was a kid. Taught me some survival skills."

"Sounds like he was training you for Search and Rescue."

Silence.

"Yes, it does. Let's cut up here." She pointed to a ridge, jutting out into the river.

Good call. He followed her up the slope, slowing,

grasping at shrubbery, finally reaching the top of the ridge.

He had passed her on the climb up, and she had fallen a little behind and only now—what an idiot—did he realize she was carrying the backpack. "Let me have that."

She bent over, breathing hard. "I got it. It's only got a soggy sandwich in it."

Right. In the meantime, he shoved his arm back into the handkerchief that she'd tied around his neck, his shoulder burning.

And that's when he saw it.

The forest where they'd left the cabin was ablaze, but she was right, the fire seemed to sit in the pocket of the gulch, not moving too fast, but definitely on the way to the movie set.

"Let's move."

They took off along the ridge, and as twilight turned dark, they slowed, heading down to the dirt road they'd taken. Here, the mountains hid the fire, save for the tiniest press of light in the distance. Then the moon rose, cast light upon them, and bled out any of the glow.

She started to run again, so he did too.

But really, all he could think was…despite the trauma, despite the crazy…he didn't want it to end.

His words in the cave stirred inside him.

"I don't think I want to be an actor anymore."

No, he didn't want to be *only* an actor anymore. Because the fact was, he liked telling stories. Liked creating the magic. And maybe even liked being the hero.

But he also liked figuring out how the magic worked. Crafting the scenes.

He slowed.

"I see the movie lights." She slowed her jog.

Indeed, a crane spilled faux moonlight onto the set of the town.

"What are they shooting tonight?"

"Blossom and Deacon have a scene outside the sheriff's office where she asks him not to fight Irish. Or at least, not to take Hawken with him."

"What are you going to do?"

He slipped his hand into hers, stopped her. Pulled her back to himself. "I'm rewriting the ending. I'm going to tell him that Hawken gets to be the hero."

"Even if he doesn't get the girl?"

"Oh, he's going to get the girl too." He winked. And then he kissed her.

If he could, he'd let time stop, sink into this moment, right here, when the hero *did* get the girl. When she kissed him back, as if the world wasn't on fire around them.

Just a moment, a delicious, perfect movie-worthy moment.

She finally pushed away. "The girl needs to alert her fire team to the fact that the *forest is burning down*."

Right, right. They turned back to the road, picking up the pace.

He was hurting and out of breath by the time they reached the set.

But, instead of Deacon and Blossom standing on the street, the light bathing them, the crew silent as they delivered their lines, Cosmos stood talking to a couple of Ember County sheriff deputies. Nearby, Indigo had her arm around Gemma. A few gaffers were taking down lights, but the cameras were off, grips stowing them.

Win and Kathryn, still in costume, stood in the craft services tent, talking.

"Shoot. I bet they're worried about us." Spenser dropped her hand, walking up to Cosmos. "Sorry! It's okay. We're back now. Everything's fine."

Cosmos turned, looked at him, frowned.

Spenser felt Emily's hand on his arm. "That's Mitch, our Incident Commander."

He stilled, glanced around, his gaze falling again on Gemma. And something inside him simply hollowed out.

"What's—"

"Bucky is missing," Cosmos said.

A beat.

"Did you search the set? Follow the cat? I mean— you know Bucky. He's—"

"Not this time, Spense." Cosmo glanced at Mitch, then back to Spenser.

Spenser gaped. "What's going on?"

"We have reason to believe that Bucky has been kidnapped."

CHAPTER 11

SPENSER HAD NEVER FELT SO HELPLESS, AND HE wasn't even related to Bucky.

But he sort of *felt* like Bucky. Because he'd been Bucky, the kid on set who was bored, or curious, or sometimes in the way. Until season three when he'd become the lead.

Then he'd just let Quillen become him.

"Are you absolutely sure Bucky didn't wander off?"

He stood in the craft services tent—shut down now for the day—with the Ember Sheriff, a man named Hutchinson, while Emily pulled her Incident Commander aside and briefed him on the fire.

Out of the corner of his eye, he saw her becoming passionate with hand gestures and pointing. As soon as they found Bucky, he'd fill the Sheriff's ear about the two gunmen in the woods.

"Yes. Gemma went to get him from the trailer, and there was a note on the table. It said— "I've taken Bucky."

"Was it signed?"

"Yeah, by Gil." Cosmos lifted his hand, wringing the back of his neck.

Gil. Who was— "The set PA? Maybe he took him to run lines—"

"Gil's the one who's been sabotaging us." This from Swen who had come out of the darkness from the SFX trailer. "We have him on camera in the house, probably dousing the curtains with spray accelerant. And the costume assistant said that he came in to get Kathryn's dress to bring it to the costume trailer."

"Gil? Skinny Gil?"

"Gil Francisco. He worked for me as an SFX assistant a couple years ago on a movie. He set up a fire scene wrong and nearly killed three people. I fired him on the spot. I didn't even see him on set until yesterday, after the barn fire. And that's when I approached Cosmos with my suspicions."

"What does he want with Bucky?" Spenser asked.

"I don't know," Swen said.

"Did you find out he took Bucky before or after you suspected him of sabotaging the set?" Spenser asked.

"After," Swen said. "Why?"

"Maybe he's onto—"

"He's back!" Gemma's voice raised across the parking lot, and she took off running as Bucky climbed down from a truck. She scooped him up in her arms.

Gil got out of the driver's side. Shut the door. "What's going on? Did someone get hurt?" He walked toward Cosmos and Swen even as Sheriff Hutchinson strode up to him.

"Where were you?"

Gil frowned, glanced at Cosmos, back to the Sheriff. "I went to town with Bucky. We had ice cream. He was wandering around the set, looking for his mom, and when I couldn't find her either, I thought maybe he'd like some ice cream. I checked with craft services, but Julia didn't have any, so we went to town."

"I was crazy with worry!" Gemma said, holding Bucky's hand, charging up to him. "What about the *note*?"

"What about the note?" Gil said. "I left it in the trailer so you knew that he was with me."

"It said, 'I took Bucky' — what kind of person writes that?" Cosmos said.

"A responsible one? Sheesh. What—wait. Did you think I *took* him? As in kidnapped him?" Gil looked at Bucky, back to Cosmos. "Why would I do that?"

"I fired you five years ago for nearly killing people on set. And now—"

"Hey." Gil held up his hand. "Yeah, you're right. I was in way over my head. But I've been working as a PA for five years. I didn't even know you were the SFX guy until I got here. And believe me, I've been trying to stay out of your way."

"Hiding is more like it. What were you doing in the house?"

Gil frowned at him. "What house?"

"The cabin that burned down a week ago," Spenser said quietly. He'd lost track of Emily in all the chaos.

"I wasn't in the house," Gil said.

"We have you on camera."

Gil just looked at him. "I have no memory of that.

I might have gone into the house when Trace was blocking his scene—I remember getting him from his trailer. But that's all."

"And you had access to Kathryn's dress. It was sprayed with accelerant."

Gil's mouth opened. "I brought it to the costume tent. Left it hanging there for her."

"Was Kathryn there?"

"No, she was…um. Wait. She was behind the tent, having a fight. I remember voices."

"With whom?"

"I don't know. I didn't stick around. A man."

A beat, and Cosmos took a breath, looked at the sheriff.

"You're fired," Swen said.

"Hey!" Gil said. "That's not fair."

Cosmos clamped him on the shoulder, his voice calm. "Sorry, Gil. Until we figure this out, we need you off the set."

"I didn't do anything!"

Cosmos nodded. "Stick around town—I promise, as soon as we clear this up, you can come back."

Gil's mouth tightened around the edges. "I quit. This movie is cursed. It's a regular Macbeth."

Everyone stilled.

"You did not just say that," Spenser said.

Gil held up his hands, backed away. Looked at the sheriff. "I'll give you my cell phone if you need to get a hold of me."

The Sheriff walked with him to his truck.

Spenser turned back to Cosmos and Swen. "You believe him?"

"I'm just glad to have Bucky back." Cosmos

looked at Spenser, gave him a once over. "What happened to you?"

Where did he start? The river? The mine? The attempt on his life?

"It's a long story." He looked around. "Have you seen Emily?"

"The firefighter? No. Maybe she's with the Ember Incident Commander."

Right. But he didn't see him, either.

"Listen, we're striking the set and moving the trailers. Just the honey wagon and the production trailer up at the house tomorrow. We have a short turn-around, and the call time is five a.m., so get some shut-eye."

Sure. Right after he found Emily. And got his leg wound looked at. It had stopped bleeding, so maybe the cut wasn't as deep as he thought. But first, he headed toward the Sheriff. "I need to talk to you," he said. "I need to report an attempted murder."

Sheriff Hutchinson turned away from Gil. "Oh?"

"A couple guys chased me and my...uh, friend into a mine today. Shot at us."

"What guys?"

"They were up by the old mine, in a cabin."

"The same cabin that exploded earlier today?"

He blinked at him. "You know about that?"

"An aerial spotter called it in. They're always doing flyovers this time of year, looking for fires. Commander Dafoe sent in his fire team earlier today to suppress it, so it's being worked on."

Maybe Emily went down to the fire station.

"I'd like to take a statement from you and your friend—"

"Emily Micah. She's a hotshot."

"Then she's probably deployed with her team."

"No, she was here just a bit ago with her Incident Commander."

"That was Commander Dafoe. He was headed up to the fire and just stopped by to make sure the crew was leaving the area. He left about ten minutes ago." A call came in over the radio, and he stepped away to respond to it.

Spenser stared out into the darkness, north, where he could just barely make out the flicker of orange.

His stomach knotted, and all he could think was, *be with her, Jesus.*

"I'll meet you at the station." The sheriff turned back to Gil.

Spenser headed to the props trailer and found some tape, then went to his trailer, took a shower, doctored the wound. Nope, not as deep as he thought, but he'd have a decent scar. Then he changed clothes, and packed up a few things—his script, a water bottle—into his satchel. Finally he went out and got on his bike. His shoulder still ached, but he could manage the bike if he took it easy.

The craft services tent was already down, the grips were loading the cameras onto trucks, the gaffers breaking down the lights.

For a second, he stood there— the sense of loss, or grief, maybe, sweeping through him. He'd had the same feeling when they'd struck the set of *Trek of the Osprey.*

As if he'd lost a piece of himself.

His words to Emily in the cave pinged back to him. *Like ten years of playing a character you desperately want to be like, only to have it end. And then you discover that you're not him. And never will be.*

But maybe he hadn't lost Quillen. Maybe Quillen was inside him.

Maybe he *was* Quillen.

I would rather sit here with the real Quillen Cleveland and finish off this pizza.

Maybe the best part of Quillen actually came from him, and he should stop trying so hard to separate them.

Oh, he was just tired. And missing Emily.

He drove into town and headed to the Ember police station.

Sheriff Hutchinson was already there and assigned a deputy to take his statement. He sat for a good hour reliving the terror of the day, offering a description of Skinny and Ponytail man to the police, along with his recollection of the explosion. They'd shown him a few pictures of local guys, former troublemakers, but he hadn't recognized any of them as the gunmen.

His stomach was furious and empty by the time he left the station. Nine p.m. The Hotline was probably still serving barbeque.

He found himself, instead, parked in front of Emily's house. The light burned inside, and he spotted movement. He sat for a second, not sure what he wanted to say to her. Wait for him? Come with him?

Maybe just…I love you? He blew out a breath. Okay, that did sound a little crazy, but…fear or faith, right?

He got off the bike and went to the door. Knocked.

No answer. He tried the knob, and the door turned. He stuck his head inside. "Emily?"

The shower was running.

He hesitated, but then stepped inside and went to the bathroom door. "Hey, Emily, I'm just here in your living room. I was thinking we could grab a bite at the Hotline."

No answer.

Her bedroom door was open—or at least he guessed it might be hers, given the yellow helmet on the dresser, her name across the brim. His gaze landed on her made bed.

No, on his face on a *massive blanket* on her made bed.

What—?

He couldn't stop himself from stepping inside the room. Staring at the blanket. *What on earth?*

"Oh, I don't think you were meant to see that."

He stilled, turned.

Her roommate JoJo stood in the doorway, dressed in shorts and a T-shirt, her hair up in a towel.

"What is this?"

"A blanket?"

He gave her a look. "Where did she—"

"It was an exclusive gift for—"

"Members of the Stormies." He let out a breath. "Only the top fans got these. The ones who subscribed to the Stormie box, the ones who attended the private fan get-togethers, and who came to Comic Con. There were only 100 of these blankets made. And she has one."

JoJo nodded. "She's a...mega fan."

His gaze fell to the bookshelf and again, he simply froze.

"She has every season of *Trek of the Osprey* on Blue ray," he said softly. "She brought it with her?"

His gaze now landed on a bobble head of Quillen on her desk and then — he stepped closer.

A picture in a frame of a much younger Emily, and a much younger Quillen, taken at a comic con, maybe ten years ago. And he'd signed it. *To Emily. The adventure awaits!*

"You okay?" JoJo said.

No. Not even a little. How had he not seen this? So many clues.

She could quote lines. Could name content from specific episodes. Did she know about his life? The stalker?

He picked up a wooden plaque on the desk. Stared at it. *Nizaagi'ian*

"What is that?" JoJo asked. "I never understood the writing."

"It's Iwoni. The word for love in a made-up language." He set the plaque down, his stomach roiling.

I would rather sit here with the real Quillen Cleveland and finish off this pizza.

"I might be sick."

And then, even as he turned and pushed past JoJo, out the door, it occurred to him.

What if Emily was the saboteur? What if she'd created the fires to make sure she could be on set?

"Spenser? Do you want to wait for her? She's at the fire house — I saw her there when our team came in."

"No." He hit the door. "Don't tell her I was here."

In fact, maybe he never was.

Probably, she should be with her team, helping fight the fire, but Emily saw the signs.

Gemma was one bad moment away from a panic attack.

Which was why, as soon as Sheriff Hutchinson tracked down Gil to get the lowdown, Emily had gone over to Gemma and asked to take her home. Where she could feel safe. Tuck Bucky into bed. Stand at his door and remind herself that her world wasn't imploding.

So, she hadn't said goodbye to Spenser, who was locked in a conversation with Cosmos and Swen, and instead directed Gemma to her car where Emily took the keys and drove her home.

Gemma sat in the back seat with Bucky, holding him.

"Mom—you're hurting me!"

And it would only get worse if Gemma didn't unwind from her trauma, her worry.

Gemma directed her to a small bungalow just a few blocks from Emily's rental. Perfect. She could walk home. And tomorrow, maybe get a ride back up to the set on Spenser's bike to retrieve her truck.

"I'm just going to walk you guys inside," Emily said as Gemma got out.

Gemma just nodded, her face white.

Something wasn't right here, she knew it in her bones.

Weeds and scrub grass grew like a jungle in the yard, bugs darting in and out of the light of a bare bulb by the door.

The unlocked door.

But then again, this was Ember.

She walked into an entryway filled with clutter—

boxes piled up by the door, and in the living room, toys and games and clothing, and more boxes. Laundry buried a sofa. "Are you moving?" Emily asked.

"I wish," Gemma said softly.

She entered the kitchen and turned on the lights. The sink was empty, the counter clean, but the trash had been stacked above the garbage can—cereal and macaroni and hamburger helper and chip bags—the debris of someone too tired to cook.

"Are you hungry, Bucky?" Emily asked.

Bucky shook his head.

"Gemma, it's late. Why don't you get him into bed?" While she tidied up a bit.

Gemma disappeared down the hallway with Bucky, and Emily found an empty grocery bag and filled it with garbage, then tied the plastic garbage bag and pulled it from the can.

She found the door to the garage and paused a moment at the debris that cluttered the space. A truck sat in the middle of the garage surrounded by bags and bags of garbage and broken furniture—a chair, a table, a lamp. In the bed of the truck was a porch swing, in pieces.

Oh boy.

She shut the door, then found more trash bags under the sink and refilled the can. Then she dumped sour milk, sitting in a gallon jug on the table, put the sticky bowl in the sink, and discovered a stash of Gatorade bottles sitting on the floor by the sliding glass door.

"That belonged to Doug, my husband. Bucky's father."

Emily stood up. "They're unopened."

"I know. It was the last thing he bought before he went to work."

"I'm so sorry." She knew he'd died—had seen the pictures at the Hotline. "How long has he been gone?"

Gemma wiped her hands on her pants, then walked over to a kitchen chair and sat down. Looked out the window. She was a pretty woman—mid-thirties, maybe, with dark hair, a few lines around her eyes. "Eight years ago. Bucky was a month old."

Emily tried not to react. To just…breathe.

Eight. Years.

"I've had a little trouble moving on." She sighed. "I started gathering his clothes a few years ago, put them in boxes, but…I don't know. I just can't get rid of them. And then there are the donations—people gave us toys and clothes for Bucky—they still do. But it feels so…I don't know. I just can't seem to figure out a way to…" She sighed. "I don't know what I would have done if Bucky was actually kidnapped. Or hurt… He's my whole life."

Emily pulled out a chair. "I know you're traumatized, Gemma, but Bucky isn't. Not right now. He doesn't know what you suspected. So, don't live there. Don't let your brain spiral out into the what ifs. What do you know is true right now?"

Gemma looked at her. Sighed. "Bucky is safe. In bed, reading. And…"

"C'mon. More. And?"

"And I'm safe too?"

"Yes, you are." She touched her arm. "A terrible thing happened to you and Bucky, and your husband. And I'm so sorry. I can imagine how difficult it's been for you to move on."

"But I want to move on. I mean—I don't want to forget him. But I feel like I'm trapped. I can't seem to let him go, but I also don't want to drown, either. And…"

"And that's what happens when all you see is the things that you lost."

She nodded.

"Okay, listen. I'm not a therapist, so I'm going to say right now that I have the name of one, and you need to get grief counseling. And therapy. But as a person who lived through trauma, I want you to know there is an exit. There is light waiting. You will get through this, and you will be free from the terrible weight of grief, at least most of the time. You will learn to live again. Even, find peace."

Even as she said it, the words settled inside.

Maybe that's what it means to be well—to know you're safe, even when you feel like you're falling.

In fact, she hadn't suffered a panic attack in… well, given she'd nearly been buried alive in a mine, and drowned in a waterfall, maybe the fact she hadn't crumbled, hadn't had the world close in seemed a lot like peace.

Maybe it's not about where you are, or what's happening around you, but who you're with.

She looked at Gemma. "Listen. You're not alone, Gemma. The firefighting community needs to know you need help. Because that's why we're here. As soon as we get this fire out, we'll be by to help you with the boxes, and the yard, and the garage—" She raised an eyebrow.

"The truck doesn't run. And the garbage cans are stuck behind the truck."

For eight years. "We can fix that too."

Tears streaked down Gemma's face. "Thank you, Emily. You should be a trauma therapist."

Emily stilled. "What?"

"Oh, I didn't mean you're not a great firefighter. Just...you seem to understand and...I guess that's a sort of gift. Thank you."

A sort of gift. "You're welcome. Let's finish cleaning this kitchen, and then I need to get back to the fire house and see if my team needs me."

"I still have Doug's radio. I know—crazy, but they never asked for it back, and sometimes I just think of his voice coming through on the other side so... anyway, they deployed the smokejumpers with the hotshots, but they got the fire routed toward the river, so they're coming back for the night."

Good. Because next on her agenda was to find Spenser.

And tell him...what? She loved him? And what good would that do—he was leaving.

But maybe she should stop looking ahead, letting the what-ifs turn her to panic. Fear or Faith?

She helped Gemma clean the kitchen, swept the floor and made her some scrambled eggs, then she walked the three blocks to her house.

The light was on, and she went inside. Music played from JoJo's room. Ben Rector. "JoJo? When did you get back?"

"Oh, Emily." JoJo came from the room, her dark hair still wet. She wore a tank top and jeans. "Spenser was here."

"He was—do you know where—"

"He saw the blanket."

She blinked at her. "What?"

"He walked into the house—I was in the shower.

He thought I was you—so I got out as fast as I could and tried to intercept him, but I found him in your room."

"The blanket was on the bed."

"His gorgeous face, right there. And he knew it was from a fan box. Apparently, one of 100?"

Oh no. "He saw the comic con picture?"

"Probably. And you have some plaque written in—

"*Nizaagi'ian*. It means I love you in Iwoni."

"Yep. That."

Oh. Okay, calm down. So, she was a fan of Quillen.

He wasn't Quillen—sure, maybe Quillen had a few of his qualities, but Spenser Storm was so much more. Flawed, honest, uncertain, brave—

Quillen was a shadow of the real man.

"Where is he?"

"I don't know. He mentioned going to the Hotline."

She should change clothes—she was still in her grimy, mine-caked, water-rumpled fire attire. No time for a shower, though.

As she changed into a pair of jeans and a T-shirt, her gaze fell on her complete collection of *Trek* seasons on blue ray. Ah, shoot.

"I'm going with you," JoJo said, meeting her in the living room. "I'll drive."

They headed out the door and got into JoJo's compact. Three blocks later, they pulled up into the lot and she spotted Spenser's bike.

Calm. Down. Don't panic.

JoJo came around the car. "I'll be at the smokejumper table if you need me."

"It'll be fine." Shoot, it came out all choked and garbled. JoJo raised an eyebrow, then turned to her.

"Ho-*kay*. Listen. Just remember. You're not a stalker. And he's just a guy. Not a super galactic hero. So, breathe."

"Breathing."

JoJo grabbed the door, walked inside, and Emily followed.

The place was loud, country music playing, a few of her fellow hotshots at a table, the Trouble Boys, with Sanchez at another. Smokejumpers in the back.

Everything normal.

Except at the bar sat Spenser, along with others from the set—Winchester Marshall, and of course Kathryn Canary. Who had her shoulder against Spenser's, her face animated as she told him a story.

And then he laughed at something she said, put his arm around her.

What?

Calm down. They were friends.

She took a breath and approached the bar. "Hey, Spenser."

He seemed to freeze, then slowly he turned. His pale blue gaze settled on her, something cool in it, his mouth a pinched line.

What…?

"What do you want?"

She blinked at him.

Kathryn leaned over him, smiled at her. "Sweetheart, we're off the set now. If you need Spenser, he has an early call—he'll see you at the shoot tomorrow."

"I don't…"

"Isn't one autograph enough?" Kathryn raised an eyebrow.

Emily looked at her, then at Spenser.

Hurt flashed in his eyes a moment before, "Actually, I don't think we need you at the set tomorrow. You've done enough. Thanks, Emily."

Then he turned his back to her.

"Wait—Spenser? What's—I don't understand."

She didn't expect him to whirl back around. To face her, cut his voice low. To tear her world into shreds. "I don't know what game you've been playing, Emily. I don't want to believe that you've been sabotaging us to get close to me, and I thank God no one was seriously injured, but I think it's best for everyone if you just…stayed away. My career is on the line here, and the last thing I need is another fiasco on set. So please, for me—if you actually care about me, and not just Quillen Cleveland—walk away."

Her eyes burned, her breath swept away.

Beside him, Kathryn slid her hand over his arm. Holding it, as if to give support. And delivered an Oscar-worthy look of pity at Emily.

Run.

She didn't even hear a different option.

She turned and pushed through the crowd, out into the night. Gulped a breath. Stars blinked down at her as she stalked through the parking lot, then out into the street.

How—how—

"Ma'am, are you okay?"

A deep voice, and for a second she thought—but no, it wasn't Spenser running after her to tell her it was all just a terribly scripted act.

Trace Wilder stuck his elbow out of his truck, slowed it, put it in park.

She stopped. "Yes, I'm fine."

He got out. "You don't look fine. You're Emily, right? From the set?"

"Yeah." She gritted her teeth, nodded. "What are you doing back in town? I thought your scenes were over."

"Oh, I was on hold, in case they needed me for any retakes." He smiled. "I'm not done until the shooting is over." He touched her arm. "Do you need a ride?"

And weirdly, it felt so terribly like that moment, as a six-year-old, running from the monster in the woods, that she simply froze.

"No," she shook her head, tried to pull away, but his grip tightened. "Hey!"

But his hand clamped over her mouth, and then he spun her around and pulled her against himself, his arm against her neck. "We have one more epic shot before this movie comes to an end," he said into her ear.

And just like that, the air left her body, and her world turned black.

CHAPTER 12

SHE WANTED OUT OF THE MOVIE BUSINESS.

Emily closed her eyes. Clearly, she was losing her mind, just a little, but that's what happened when a girl sat duct-taped to a hard backed chair for six hours in the attic of the abandoned house of the finale scene of *The Drifters*.

The long night had allowed her lots and lots of empty time to consider her stupidity. Yes, Spenser might have been a jerk, but she'd been wrong not to tell him about her epic level of fan commitment. She knew about the stalker, knew he was a little sensitive to, um, overzealous fans. But she'd been so...normal.

Mostly normal.

She'd only quoted a few lines. And she hadn't asked him, not even once, to speak Iwoni.

Certainly, he knew that her feelings for him weren't...well, weren't about Quillen.

Except, of course he clearly *hadn't* known because, as she rolled film of their moments together in her hours and hours of empty time, she saw herself quoting the shows and calling him Quillen and generally fangirling all over him.

She'd push her away, too.

And yes, it hurt that he'd thought she'd sabotaged the set, but even that, painfully, made sense.

Although, she *hadn't* sabotaged the set.

Trace Wilder had, although she hadn't a clue why. Hard to ask questions when a guy knocked you out and then, you know, *taped your mouth shut*. He'd left her there in the thick of the night too, giving her a beautiful view of the attic window, out of which she watched the stars and tried to remember her father's survival tips.

She'd managed to turn her wrists red and raw from trying to work out of the duct tape securing them to the sides of the chair. Her ankles were no better. She had managed to loosen them a little, but he'd wrapped the tape so much, she hadn't a prayer of breaking free.

She had made progress on the tape over her mouth, but not enough to shout through a closed, albeit broken window, and down three stories to the gaffers and grips who arrived at O'dark thirty to set up for today's scene.

Certainly, someone would come upstairs. Please!

But no. Apparently, the scene, an epic shootout — and she knew this from reading the script — would be shot entirely outside.

She'd read the script, as well as the Scene Breakdown. A beautiful ending where Deacon Cooper and Hawken face down the bad guys, and Deacon dies while trying to rescue Blossom and Dusty from the house.

Blossom and Dusty are thrown as the house explodes, and her guess was that's when she'd die too, so, that was an exciting finale. Because she had no doubt that Trace had tampered with the cannons that would create the explosion.

The house, of course, wasn't really *supposed* to explode—just a massive explosion out of the front door while Dusty and Blossom ran away. But surprise, surprise, the house would go up in flames, then they would turn, holding each other as they looked back in horror.

So much horror.

And Hawk would join them in a final epic shot.

She would have liked to see that shot. She bet Spenser would nail it, and maybe that made her even more pitiful.

She wasn't even angry at him.

The final scene would be the epilogue a year later when Hawk and Blossom would ride to town, Dusty in the wagon, Blossom pregnant with the next generation of Coopers.

And everyone would swoon.

The sun's rays cast into the room, orange and gold, the light of morning just clearing the eastern peaks. It was magic hour, and any moment now, Cosmos—or rather, Indigo, would shout 'Quiet on the set,' then 'Speed,' and 'Action,' and the ending would begin.

Yes, she might be losing her touch with reality a little. But really, how could it be that she'd found herself exactly in the place of her nightmares?

Breathe.

She just had to make enough noise for someone to hear her. Now, along with the gaffers and grips, the cameramen and ADs had arrived, the PAs and costume assistants, the prop people, the craft services tent, and all the extras from Irish's crew that played the villains.

Even Kathryn and Spenser and Winchester—she spotted Win outside talking with Indigo. Cosmos, checking camera angles. The boom man holding the mic.

It was a virtual city outside. Certainly, *someone* would find her.

She just had to make noise.

If only Trace hadn't shoved her into the *attic*.

Then of course, there was the small issue that her feet couldn't touch the ground. She swayed back and forth, harder, harder—yes, the chair thumped.

Pitiful.

She put a little more oomph into it. Thumped again.

Better.

She thumped again. There, certainly someone—

Bam! She went over, shoulder slamming onto the floor. Heat spiked up her arm, and she groaned.

That felt thunderous. *C'mon!*

Please! Hello! No one?

She lay there, listening to the voices outside. For the love.

She closed her eyes.

Don't panic.

Maybe it's not about where you are, or what's happening around you, but who you're with.

Spenser. His words in the cave. But, right. Yes.

Please, Jesus, be here with me.

Footsteps sounded on the stairs.

She loved a fast reply.

"Mmm!" She had tried to loosen the tape with her

tongue but had gotten nowhere. She thumped on the floor. "Mmm!"

More steps and she tried to bang her shoulder. *Here! In here!*

The doorknob turned, and she held her breath.

And then, Bucky opened the door. He wore a pair of jeans, a dirty shirt, his hair mussed, ready for his shot. He stood in the doorway, just stared at her.

"Mmm!" She wriggled hard.

His mouth opened.

C'mon Bucky. Shout, or come over here. Do *something.*

"Bucky! Come down here!" Kathryn, her voice from below, maybe the first floor.

No—no—

Bucky turned and closed the door. Footsteps sounded, running down the stairs.

What...wait!

Aw, Bucky.

She gritted her jaw, refused tears.

Now what? She closed her eyes.

Breathe.

Don't panic.

Five. Five things she saw. She opened her eyes. The door, with the half-broken, dented knob. The ceiling, cobwebs in the corners. Peeling yellow wallpaper, so maybe once upon a time, this had been a bedroom. Mouse droppings. That was nice. And...five...five— there, on the floor in the corner, an old high-heeled shoe.

Four things she could feel. That was easy— tingling in her fingers, the raw burn of her wrists, pain shooting down her arm. Her lips, cracked and dry, and...

Tears dripping into her ears.

"Quiet on the set!" Indigo's voice lifted in the hush of the set.

She closed her eyes. Three things to hear.

"Speed!"

She imagined the shout of 'Action,' because popping sounded, the squibs exploding. Shouts outside, voices of extras protecting the house. More squibs.

A scream—probably Kathryn.

The thunder of her heartbeat swishing in her ears.

Smell. Two things to smell.

Well, she wasn't smelling too rosy after her day in the mine. Maybe she should have had that shower.

And then, dust. So much of it. Which meant the wood was old. It would ignite fast, like a burning bush.

Probably not the best thought, because now she'd have to start over with the five.

She swallowed. No. She refused to believe she was alone.

She closed her eyes. And there she was, back in Missouri, at a house. Her house. Her mother was in the den, just getting off the phone, and her father— her adopted father Jim Micah held her in his arms. *"Daddy, take me riding?"*

"Have you ever been on a horse before?"

"No. Don't let me fall, okay?"

He laughed, his blue eyes shiny. "I won't honey. Daddy won't let you fall, I promise."

She opened her eyes. *Maybe that's what it means to be well—to know you're safe, even when you feel like you're falling.*

Because Daddy wouldn't let her fall.

And then, as she lay there, she felt as if two hands came over her shoulders. Gripped.

Held her.

Her breath caught.

The presence of Jesus. Maybe that's what makes your soul well.

Yes.

As the squibs exploded, she tasted it, the sweetness of something she couldn't explain.

Hope.

What—?

But hope swept over her, through her, her entire body filled with it.

"Fire in the hole!"

Oh, God, catch me!

Focus.

Spenser walked back to the craft services table, grabbed a bottle of water while Swen set up the shot for the final explosion.

The morning sun spread out over the far mountains like gold, pouring into the valleys— turning the pines a deep, lush green. The scent of smoke lingered in the air from yesterday, and a cloud of black lifted from behind the hill where the house sat.

So, the fire must still be burning.

Maybe Emily was fighting it, because she wasn't at home. Not last night after he'd left the Hotline, sick to his stomach after turning his back on her.

What. A. Jerk.

Even now, as he took a swig of water, he felt the

punch, saw the look on her face. But he'd been angry, felt betrayed.

And it didn't help that Kathryn seemed to stir his feelings to a boil. She'd been sitting at the bar, and the minute he walked in and sat down, she cozied up. Asked him why he looked so upset.

The story came spilling out.

She then told her own story of a crazy fan, and he'd tried to laugh, but really—

Emily was just a fan. Not crazy.

And so what if she loved Quillen? Like she said, one of three billion.

But her comment kept rounding back to him.

I would rather sit here with the real Quillen Cleveland and finish off this pizza.

The real Quillen Cleveland.

And that was it, wasn't it? He'd fought the stereotype for so many years.

But he was the prototype. He created the character out of his own personality. Just because he'd grown up into Quillen on the show didn't mean he couldn't embrace Quillen in reality.

So maybe he *was* the real Quillen Cleveland.

Maybe in a way, Quillen's quest to find his dad was your own quest to say goodbye to yours.

Yes, and more. Without his dad, he'd had no one but Quillen, and the scriptwriters—and yes, Chanel and his grandfather—but really, just he and Quillen to navigate the way. So maybe Quillen had also helped him grow up.

And that's what he'd wanted to tell her when he drove by her dark house an hour later. But it was late, and they'd had a doozy of a day.

Still, he'd hoped…

But when he'd arrived at the set, no Emily. He'd spent two hours in makeup and blocking, and by the time the sun rose and they took their magic hour shoot, he'd realized the truth.

He'd really screwed up.

On set, Swen and his crew were checking the big cannons hidden on the porch. They'd explode as soon as Blossom and Dusty cleared the house in a cinematic shot where they were rescued by—*oh no.*

And that's when he heard Cosmos.

"Okay, Winchester, ready for your big scene?"

Winchester stood in costume near Indigo.

He'd forgotten to ask about the script change.

Clearly too late. Or— "Cosmos, can I have a second?" Spenser set his water down and walked over. "What would you say about Deacon getting the girl?"

Cosmos ran a finger and thumb through his eyes. "Not you too?"

"What?"

"Trace said the same thing on his first day on set. He said that Hawk should die—he didn't deserve a happy ending." He looked at him. "Why? And you couldn't have said something during our table read?"

"Trace said Hawk should die?"

"Yes. But I just thought it was, you know, jealousy because you got his role."

Spenser stared at him. "He was cast for Hawk?"

"Originally, yes." Cosmos glanced at Win. "Actually, your agent sent a tape of a scene you did in *Trek* that Trace was in. I'm not sure if he did it to compare, but he was a guest star, and in that scene, you killed him. So maybe it was payback." Cosmos laughed.

Spenser didn't. "He was also in *Say You Love Me*."

Cosmos frowns.

"The movie I did after *Trek*. He had a role. But of course, it was never finished, so…"

Win was frowning at him. "Are you saying that Trace has a beef with you?"

"I don't know. But Kathryn said something to me last night that keeps sticking in my brain—she was in some sort of music video that Oaken Fox did earlier this week. And that Trace was in it, too."

"Yeah, he was," Win said. "I saw him a couple days ago with Kathryn. I think they have—or had—a little something going on. I spotted them fighting behind the costume tent the night she caught fire. Maybe he came back to mend fences."

"He was here with the insurance guys—he was one of the investors," Cosmos said slowly. "If he insured his investment, he'd get his money back if it went south."

"Why would he sabotage his own movie?"

Silence. A beat and then, "Me," Spenser said. "His career tanked for a while after *Say You Love Me*."

"Do you think he saw Kathryn kiss you after the barn fire?"

"Maybe. But that was after the fight in the tent."

"Could be a guy who is jealous of Spenser Storm might try and kill him…and maybe even the woman who broke his heart. And then, when that didn't work, maybe sabotage the movie." Cosmos met Spenser's gaze. "Where is Kathryn?"

"In the costume trailer, getting retouched for the finale," Indigo said.

"Get her out here—"

Boom!

Behind them the cannons fired. Plumes of gas and fire ignited, and black smoke billowed out. Indigo had ducked, along with Winchester, and a few of the cameramen ran back.

The flame spit out sparks onto the grass, igniting it, and a couple of the special effects guys ran up and stomped them out.

"Swen, shut it off!" Cosmos yelled. "Where's our hotshot?"

Aw, that was Spenser's fault. "She's—"

"I saw her upstairs." Bucky stood near the craft services table, holding a donut. "She's all tied up."

Spenser turned, looked at him. Tiny flecks of powdered sugar spilled down his chin, onto his costume. "What did you say?"

"Emily. She's upstairs." He gestured to the house. "I saw her. I didn't think she was in the movie, but..." he raised a shoulder.

Spenser looked back at the house.

Wait.

The front porch was still burning, fire now spitting out of the canister.

"Swen! Turn off the fire!" Cosmos yelled.

Swen stood holding the radio. "I did. The fire is out."

"Clearly not!"

"Hoses!"

Except, Emily wasn't here—and now that did feel strange because she'd been fired twice and still had shown up.

Spenser turned back to Bucky. "Where in the house?"

Bucky pointed to the top of the house, the attic area. "The bad guys got her."

He looked at Cosmos, who seemed to be wrapping his brain around Bucky's words too. Then he took off for the house.

"Spenser!"

The porch was engulfed, sparks still igniting from the cannon. Someone must have filled it with tinder.

He ran around the back of the house. No door — what house only had a front door?

He peered into a first story window.

The fire had burned through the door, to the stairway.

"Call the fire department!"

He backed up. "Emily! Em!"

Nothing from the top floor.

But the house was a tinder box. By the time the Jude County Fire Department got here, it would be all over.

Smoke plumed into the sky, and in a moment, the first floor blazed.

He backed up, ran back to the grips. "I need a ladder! Or a dolly!"

"Nothing we have will reach the attic," said one of the grips.

Fire kicked out of the bottom window.

"Go up the pipe." Bucky had come up beside him. "Like Quillen did when he sneaked aboard the Star Finder. He went up the garbage chute."

Spenser looked at him. "You watch *Trek*?"

"Emily and I watched it on set, in my trailer. She has all the shows."

Yeah, she did.

"Tell Rocco to get the biggest Stunt Pit he can find."

"Spenser," Cosmos said, but Spenser ignored him.

The drain pipe. Not the flimsy metal of today, but a real metal pipe attached to the house, all the way to the roof.

He put his hands on it — not hot yet — and hoisted himself up, fixed his boots on either side of the pipe, then worked his way up — hands, then feet, then hands — past the flaming first floor, to the second, the ground falling away fast, his heartbeat propelling him up.

Hang on, Emily.

He reached the second floor and shoved open a window. Smoke billowed out. He pulled a breath then launched himself inside.

The flames hadn't yet reached the second floor, but they were climbing the stairs. His eyes burned as he spotted the stairs to the attic.

Please, Bucky, be right.

He thundered up the narrow stairs and grabbed the knob. It rattled in his grip, but the door opened.

His knees nearly buckled. Emily lay on her side, taped to a chair, struggling, tape over her mouth.

What — ?

He scrambled over to her and carefully peeled the tape from her mouth.

She gulped in a breath, then another. Then, "Hi."

"What — how — "

"Trace. He grabbed me last night — " Her eyes widened. "Shut the door!"

He turned, and smoke had followed him up, now sneaking through the door. He shut it, then came back, fighting with her tape.

"It's too much. You need a knife. Or — wait — by the floor. Get that shoe!"

He turned and spotted the shoe. A lone stiletto.

"Pull the heel guard off."

He fought with it for a second before it ripped free. Under it was a metal spike.

"Got it." He held the tape and began to rip at it with the spike. It frayed then separated, and in a moment, he'd ripped off the tape from one wrist, then the other.

Then, her ankles.

She scrambled free of the chair, got to her knees. Looked at him, her eyes reddened.

"You came for me."

He swallowed, nodded. "Of course I came for you. I love you, Emily."

Her eyes filled. "Oh—" Her hand pressed her mouth. "I'm so sorry, Spenser. I should have told you about… I'm a Stormie. I have the badge and the pins and the—"

"Blanket."

"Yeah. I really like the blanket. It's soft, and it's got a nice face on it." She wrinkled her nose. "But I should have told you."

"I'm not sure what's so terrible about falling for a woman who's my biggest fan. I'm sorry, Emily. I shouldn't have—"

She launched herself into his arms, hers tight around his neck, her body hard against his.

Oh.

But okay, this worked. His arms circled her. "Shh. We're going to be okay. It's okay. I'll get you out of here."

She leaned back then, her gaze in his, his face in her hands. "Of course you will."

And then she kissed him, her mouth hungry, her touch demanding, no fear, all possession.

Now this was a hostage situation he could get behind.

She let him go too quickly, but maybe, since the house was on fire— "More of that later," she said and pushed off him. "Let's get out of here."

Right.

He went to the window.

She went to the door. "The doorknob is hot."

"Rocco is outside with the pit."

Her eyes widened. "What?"

"The crash mat—it's called a stunt pit."

"You want us to *jump*?" She came over to the window, which he'd opened and now stuck her head out beside his.

Below them, the stunt team, along with a few grips, had moved a massive pad under the window.

"No. Uh-uh. Not happening." She pulled her head back in. Looked at him.

"Just pretend it's episode 201."

She stared at him. "Escape from planet Ninov? Quillen jumped from a tower into a pile of Lightweave."

"*I* jumped into the Lightweave. I was doing my own stunts by then. Listen. You'll jump, then in midair, turn and just fall on your back, arms out. Let the mat take your weight."

"You're kidding, right?" She looked out the window. "I'm not throwing my body out three stories."

"It's not that far."

"No."

He took her by the shoulders. "Listen. I want you to take all that fear and bottle it up and put it deep inside and let it fuel you. Let it make you strong, and

179

brave, and remind you that you have everything you need inside you to do big things. Impossible things. Inspiring things. You were made to do these things, Kaylen. You just have to believe."

A beat. "Quillen's speech to his little brother, when he leaves him behind."

"Yeah. Except, I'm actually going to follow you out of the window. But it still works, right?"

She made a face. "A little."

"How about this—you're the bravest woman I know. So please jump out the window so we can live happily ever after."

"That's the one." She moved to the window, even as smoke seeped through the door. "Just jump."

"Land on your back. Arms out. I'll be right behind you."

She ducked her head and climbed out of the window. Shouts below as she stood on the sill.

"The adventure awaits!"

"Very funny!" But she pushed off.

Screamed.

Then she turned, midair, like he told her, and landed with a whoof onto the mat.

Fire now licked the floor, the edges of the door, smoke gusting in.

He put a leg out of the window, ducked under the sill.

Smoke from the lower windows poured out and behind him, the door cracked, gave way.

Fire leaped into the room, across the rafter.

Wow, he was tired of escaping burning buildings.

With a shout, he pushed off, into the air, flying. *The adventure awaits!*

CHAPTER 13

WHAT A RUSH.

And not just the sense of jumping off a building, but…the falling.

The being caught.

The adrenaline of not just surviving, but living.

Emily watched as her hotshot team sprayed water on the house, now engulfed in flames. Droplets fell in the saturated air like a sort of baptism.

Fear or faith. Both. The fear could make her smart. The faith could make her bold.

And at the end of it, God would catch her.

Maybe Spenser would be there too, because he stood behind her, his arms locked around her, his head on hers, watching the fire die.

"They'll probably want a statement," Spenser said softly.

"Yeah." She glanced at the sheriff's police cruiser where Trace Wilder sat in the back seat. "I wish I'd seen Winchester tackle him."

"Me too. But Win did miss our epic jump."

"No worries, the camera caught everything."

She glanced over at the voice. Cosmos, his arms folded, watching the fire eat his prop. "Really?"

"It was a great stunt. I'm going to figure out how to put it in the movie. If I can." He glanced over. "After we rewrite the ending. Good instincts there, Spenser. You should be a producer, the way you know story and set life."

Spenser made a sound, something of agreement.

"Deacon gets the girl?" Emily looked up at him.

"Only in the movie." Spenser smiled down at her.

"I think I mentioned no movie set romances," Cosmos said.

"This is the real thing," Spenser said.

The real thing. She wrapped her hands around his strong arms. The real thing.

Then she turned, put her hands on his chest. "Are you sure? I mean, we were just in a fire. Very dramatic. Maybe…"

"Sheesh. What does a guy have to do to convince you that he's in love with you?" He met her gaze. "Nizaagi'ian."

"I knew you could speak Iwoni!"

"Yeah. I'm pretty much fluent. But you know, I was pretty bored on set, so…"

"I love you, Spenser Storm. Not Quillen, although maybe you'll always be a little bit of a space cowboy in my heart, and not because you're a movie star. But because you're sweet and kind and brave, and you make *me* brave. With you, I feel safe."

"Even in the middle of a fire?"

"Mostly safe." She winked. Raised up on her toes —

"Micah!"

Oh. She lowered herself back down and spotted

the voice, coming from Conner, who was striding over to her, wearing his hard hat and yellow shirt, a grim expression.

Spenser let her go. "What's going on?"

"Commander Dafoe is calling a meeting. We got a call of the fire we set down yesterday stirring back to life and headed for a nearby ranch. We need all hotshots on hand and that means you too, Emily."

"She just jumped out of a burning house!"

Conner drew in a breath.

Oh, perfect. She looked at Spenser. "It was part of the movie. Great scene. Epic." She slid her hand down to Spenser's, took it, and squeezed.

"What about her statement to the police?"

"It'll have to wait. We're leaving the trouble crew here to finish up with the house—you and Houston and Dakota come with me." He looked at Spenser. Then, after a moment, nodded. "I think Jim will like you enough."

Then he walked away.

"Jim?"

"Conner is my godfather. He's talking about my dad." She turned to him and put her arms around his neck. "I gotta go."

"I know."

"And so do you. You have to finish your movie."

He sighed. "Yeah. Cosmos will have to shoot the finale on the backlot." He touched his forehead to hers. "But I'll be back in Montana as soon as we finish, I promise."

She nodded, the smoke biting her eyes.

"Want me to swear on the Star of Elianna—"

She kissed him, her arms around his neck, holding onto her favorite hero, lost in the magic of her happy ending. She got the hero, and the man, and...

And it was well, very well, with her soul.

He kissed her well, no acting about it, and when she let him go, he nodded, something sweet in his eyes. "Go, save the galaxy."

"One world at a time." She winked, then ran to catch up to Conner.

Thank you for reading *Flashpoint*! Gear up for the next Chasing Fire: Montana romantic suspense thriller, *Flashover* by Megan Besing. Turn the page for a sneak peek!

SECRETS. BETRAYAL. SACRIFICE.
THIS TIME, THEY'RE NOT JUST
FIGHTING FIRE.

She never expected her second chance to show up...

When her special ops brother was killed, Sophie Lamb left everything — and everyone — behind to start over. Now the owner of a ranch that rescues neglected horses, they've become her entire life. And sure, she's still haunted by the death of her brother, but she doesn't have time to miss those she's lost — including her high school crush, Houston James, who she absolutely never thinks about. Okay, almost never.

In the middle of a wildfire...

Houston James can't catch a break. Sure, he survived a house fire, and became a youth pastor, but a recent false accusation in ministry has sent him into a summer fighting fires. The last thing he expects is to find the girl he can't forget...

When the blazing Montana wildfire threatens her ranch, Sophie refuses to abandon her rescued animals. But the last person she expects to show up and demand her evacuation is of course, Houston James.

Then her prized stallion goes missing, and she and Houston must work together to track him down before the fire catches up to them. And when they stumble upon a shocking discovery, they are forced to work together, and confront their heartbreaking past, if they hope to survive.

In this relentless fight against external threats and the ghosts of their pasts, Houston and Sophie stand on the brink of a second chance. But the fight isn't over when the threat she left behind finds her...now, what will her second chance at love cost her?

Don't miss out on this gripping tale of survival and redemption in the heart-pounding second installment of the Chasing Fire: Montana series.

FLASHOVER

CHASING FIRE: MONTANA | BOOK 2

CHAPTER 1

Sophie Lamb should've never said yes. Now she would have to stand here and watch someone get killed riding one of her horses.

The sunrise soared over the roofs of the staged western town and glistened on the camera screens, which failed to catch the scent of ash in the air or the two-week-old wildfire smoke still swelling behind them. Unlike the hushed crowd around her, Sophie wasn't there to get a peek at Hollywood's latest stars reshooting a scene. She was there mainly for Thunderbolt. Her most cantankerous black stallion. The one she'd for sure advised the director not to use.

"And...action."

At the director's command, Sophie curled her toes in the pointed ends of her dusty cowboy boots. *"Come on, boy. Just one good take."*

Thunderbolt's rider, the recently upgraded extra named Jonah, leaned forward in his saddle. Holding on to his Stetson with one hand and the reins in the other, he had Thunderbolt galloping in hot. Too hot.

A trail of dust paraded behind as Thunderbolt's hooves pounded the dry ground. The clouded air tickled Sophie's throat, but she dared not make a sound to ruin the take.

They flew past the trading post, then the church. Another few heartbeats and they'd reach their mark beside two of her other horses tied to a wooden post out in front of the set's bank.

Sophie squeezed past one of the production assistants sipping coffee and zeroed in on Thunderbolt's movements. His front leg had healed quicker than Sophie's weak ankle, but he still needed slow and steady just as they'd practiced a million times before everything blew up on set the two weeks before.

Literally.

But Thunderbolt's ears weren't pulled back. He wasn't groaning. Wasn't limping.

Sophie slowed her own gait and slipped in behind one of the assistant directors in the front row of the crowd.

Maybe this speed and paired rider would work. For one take.

Jonah yanked back on the reins. Hard. Thunderbolt stopped ten feet from the desired mark. Dust swirled and went straight for the other actors, making Kathryn Canary, the lead actress, cough.

"Cut!" Cosmos Ferguson, the director, stomped toward the filming scene. "Jonah! Didn't I tell you to pull up closer to the other horses? This should have taken one take."

Jonah dropped the reins onto his lap and lifted his hands. "You think this stupid thing listens to me?"

Sophie scowled. Great. She'd been assured Jonah

was an experienced rider. Thunderbolt snorted and lifted his right front leg. Sophie pushed back her shoulders and marched across the boundary line toward Jonah.

However, Cosmos intercepted her. "Problem?"

In front of Sophie, Jonah fanned his face with his stiff Stetson as he laughed loudly into his cell phone.

Thunderbolt's left ear twitched.

Sophie nodded her head in the direction of Thunderbolt and Jonah. "That pairing is never going to work. However, I think Jonah could ride Pudding or even Chestnut. Goldie too if—"

Cosmos held up his palm. "Jonah's character must be on the darkest horse. The animal he rides is more than his transportation. It's the outer expression of the story's mood at this point of the movie."

No character's mood was worth Thunderbolt getting hurt. Or worse. He'd already been through enough trauma before she'd rescued him. All her horses had in one way or another deserved a better life. "Right. I understand that. Except..."

From on top of Thunderbolt, Jonah moved his arm through the air to something he said over his phone, and his hat flew out of his grip. The Stetson twisted into the air and dropped. But gravity didn't allow it to simply land on the ground. That would have been too easy.

Instead, it smacked against Thunderbolt's lifted leg.

He released a neigh. He reared back, eyes wide and ears flat.

Not again.

Sophie raised her hands. "Whoa, Thunderbolt. Easy."

But the only easy thing about the morning so far had been arriving on time.

The horse shot off, derby race style. Jonah hollered. His fingers reached for the reins but missed as he clung to his phone. His feet bucked in the air, as his boots weren't in the stirrups. The man couldn't even pretend to be a cowboy. "Someone stop this thing!"

If only Sophie could have pulled both of her horse trailers here and brought Daisy and Frank along too. Even Peanut. Then she could have galloped after Thunderbolt and Jonah.

Sophie put her fingers in her mouth and whistled. Thunderbolt twisted his ears back but sprinted on through the opening between two wooden set buildings.

Spencer Storm, one of the actors off scene, spurred Sophie's horse Goldie into action and took off after Thunderbolt. At least someone hadn't lied about his horse experience. Once he caught up to the pair, he grabbed Thunderbolt's reins and steered everyone back toward the cheering crowd.

As Sophie ran to intercept, Jonah yelled something, but Sophie's gaze snagged on a man wearing a navy baseball cap who walked behind the set's bank building.

She stutter-stepped, and it had nothing to do with her old ankle injuries.

The man's height resembled her brother's. So did his dark hair and nose profile.

"Crispin."

But the man didn't stop.

She took two steps after him. "Crispin!"

The man's shoulders seemed about the same size

as Crispin's. Though, the closer she got, the more he looked different from her memories. Too thin. He had a beard and wore cargo pants. Maybe it wasn't her brother. But then again, anyone could change in three years.

She sure had.

Once more, he didn't stop, and what was she thinking? Her brother had been declared dead. Even if she didn't believe it. No matter that Homeland Security kept affirming it. Regardless of what she believed, her special ops brother wasn't going to show up on the set of a movie. She didn't have the power to wish him or anyone into existence.

However, it seemed her heart, rather than her head, was in control of her feet as she jogged in the man's direction until Jonah and Spencer rode up.

Red faced, Jonah spat. He jumped down from Thunderbolt and blocked her view. "Your horse tried to kill me."

Her fingers fisted, and she bit back a retort to Jonah while her gaze returned to the alleyway. It was empty.

She swallowed a longing that surprised her. Clearly, deep inside she still clung to a fragment of hope that her brother was alive.

Cosmos marched up beside Jonah and folded his arms. "Your hat spooked this horse, and I don't believe cell phones are props for any of our western scenes."

Jonah had the decency to look guilty.

The director didn't ease his glare. "You either ride a horse, or you're out of my movie. I don't care that my godfather owes your great-aunt a favor."

Jonah held the director's gaze for three of

Sophie's thundering heartbeats before he said, "Not. That. One."

Poor Thunderbolt. It wasn't his fault. Sophie could load up all her horses and be done with the stress. But she wanted to be able to rescue more horses one day. Needed enough money to build five more barns. Or at least the one she had her bank loan application in for. For that, she needed this gig.

She slid next to Spencer and took Thunderbolt's reins from the movie star. "Thank you so much. I'm so sorry. Thunderbolt likes to run from his problems."

The slightest smile lit up Spencer's face. "Been there, done that. In fact, it was pretty much just a couple weeks ago."

Sophie nodded. "I heard about that."

According to rumors around the town of Ember, Spencer's now girlfriend, a hotshot firefighter, had been kidnapped and tied up in a burning house. But then again, rumors could spread quicker than the forest fire blazing in the distance. Sophie's past was proof of that.

Jonah grunted.

Sophie stroked Thunderbolt's cheek and then ran her palm down his leg. Nothing appeared broken, other than her latest attempt at fundraising for the ranch.

She took a deep breath. She should have also brought Daisy from the beginning, but she hated leaving Peanut and Frank alone at the barn. "I have one more horse back at the ranch that might work. Daisy is mostly black. Has white markings on her head and two spots on her feet."

Cosmos studied Jonah. "Can Daisy handle a rider who *will* listen better to your instructions?"

Jonah snarled but didn't deny anything.

"Daisy was a trail horse. She has a good and patient temperament." Maybe a bit too dormant. When her owner passed, his son assumed there was something wrong with the aged horse and had wanted to ship her off to a meat-processing facility in Mexico. Sophie had gotten a tip about the transaction and drove hours to bring the malnourished horse safely to her ranch.

Cosmos checked his watch. "If the weather and fire cooperate, we'll need Daisy here as soon as possible. We were already supposed to be heading to the backlot by now. I'll make sure someone who knows what they're doing looks after Pudding and Chestnut and the rest of your horses at the set livery while you're gone."

"That would be great."

She spotted another familiar face behind the director. This time, her eyes weren't playing tricks on her. A pile of auburn curls and a hot pink headband sat on top of Marley's head. Her best friend carried an arrangement of flowers that seemed almost as heavy as Thunderbolt's saddle. Marley's oversized overall pants rubbed together as she walked, making whooshing sounds that harmonized with the water sloshing around in the glass vase in her arms.

When Marley spotted Sophie, her smile matched the cheerfulness of the yellow roses amongst the green foliage, which Marley always called the backdrop for the flower stars. "Do you know where *the* Kathryn Canary is?"

Sophie glanced over her shoulder for the actress. Her gaze snagged once more on the empty alleyway set beside the bank and then moved on toward the vacant casting chairs. "Maybe try her dressing room? Or I think I saw her assistant over by the food table before the last take."

Marley's eyes lit up over the top layer of roses. "An assistant would be way less intimidating."

Sophie bumped her shoulder into Marley's as they headed in the direction of both the food and livery. "Now's the perfect time to meet your favorite actress. What have I told you—"

"Yes, yes, movie stars are people too, I know. But knowing that still doesn't make my words stop stuttering. I'm just glad you're still here. I wish I'd known though; I would have brought you a smoothie."

Thunderbolt blew out a breath, and Sophie patted his side as they walked. "Thanks for the thought, nonetheless. This one is in timeout, and I've got to go get Daisy."

Marley wrinkled her nose, causing her freckles to bunch together. "Thunderbolt, you need to stop being a stinker. But everyone will love to meet sweet Daisy. I still can't believe someone would send her to the glue factory."

Sophie put her hands over Thunderbolt's ears. "We don't say G.L.U.E. around the horses."

Marley laughed until her smile slipped away as they neared the food table where a group of extras dressed as cowboys pointed to the sky behind Thunderbolt.

Sophie turned along with Marley. Smoke soared above the tree line, blocking the mountain view in the distance.

Marley shifted the vase of flowers. "Hope they get the fire under control soon."

"I'm sure the firefighters will." They had to. Her ranch wasn't too far from where the fire had been heading the past few days.

A laugh floated over to them from one of the massive production trailers with a door marked "wardrobe department." Kathyrn tucked a section of her blonde hair behind her ear as she spoke to her assistant.

Sophie nodded toward the women. "In case you didn't know, Kathryn Canary is the one in the pink dress. Her assistant is in the jeans."

"Thanks, girl. Be safe driving back. Call me later. We'll set dinner plans, complete with smoothies."

"Perfect." Sophie waved bye and weaved Thunderbolt around a section of lighting and props. As she neared her horse trailer parked beside the livery barn, a red convertible blocked her hitch. She would have sighed if it would have done any good. Instead, she glanced back to the parking lot. At least her truck wasn't blocked in. She'd have to use her old trailer at home to bring Daisy back.

She pulled Thunderbolt toward the outside corral. "Looks like you're not coming home with me quite yet, boy."

A flash of blue over her shoulder in the parking lot stole Sophie's attention. A man holding an orange — one of her brother's favorite fruits — and a cell phone stood beside the Kalispell Sound and Light semi-truck.

"Crispin." Her voice came out shakier than the yell she intended.

The man paused.

Sophie stopped walking, and Thunderbolt's nose bumped into her. But the man in the navy T-shirt simply offered her a chin nod, slid his phone in his pocket, and peeled his orange before hopping into the truck. Perhaps she'd gotten less sleep than she thought last night, worrying about the smell of smoke lingering in the air when she had locked up her barn. The man was probably a film set worker.

Of course he was.

Thunderbolt snorted.

Sophie clicked her tongue and tugged his leads forward toward the set livery. "Yes, you're right, a little scenery change will do me good. And you better be on your best behavior while I fetch Daisy."

She needed to stop hoping. She couldn't keep wishing to change the past. Even if today was the third anniversary of her brother's supposed death.

Looking for more more exciting romantic suspense from Sunrise Publishing?

DON'T MISS ANY CHASING FIRE: MONTANA STORIES

With heart-pounding excitement, gripping suspense, and sizzling (but clean!) romance, the CHASING FIRE: MONTANA series, brought to you by the incredible authors of Sunrise Publishing, including the dynamic duo of bestselling authors Susan May Warren and Lisa Phillips, is your epic summer binge read.

Immerse yourself in a world of short, captivating novels that are designed to be devoured in one sitting. Each book is a standalone masterpiece, (no story cliffhangers!) although you'll be craving the next one in the series!

Follow the Montana Hotshots and Smokejumpers as they chase a wildfire through northwest Montana.

The pages ignite with clean romance and high-stakes danger—these heroes (and heroines!) will capture your heart. The biggest question is...who will be your summer book boyfriend?

A BREED APART: LEGACY UNLEASHED!

Experience the high-octane thrills, danger, and romance in Ronie Kendig's A Breed Apart: Legacy series.

SCAN OUR QR CODE FOR MORE ROMANTIC SUSPENSE!

ABOUT SUSAN MAY WARREN

With nearly 2 million books sold, critically acclaimed novelist Susan May Warren is the Christy, RITA, and Carol award-winning author of over ninety-five novels with Tyndale, Barbour, Steeple Hill, and Summerside Press. Known for her compelling plots and unforgettable characters, Susan has written contemporary and historical romances, romantic-suspense, thrillers, rom-com, and Christmas novellas.

With books translated into eight languages, many of her novels have been ECPA and CBA bestsellers, were chosen as Top Picks by *Romantic Times*, and have won the RWA's Inspirational Reader's Choice contest and the American Christian Fiction Writers Book of the Year award. She's a three-time RITA finalist and an eight-time Christy finalist.

Publishers Weekly has written of her books, "Warren lays bare her characters' human frailties, including fear, grief, and resentment, as openly as she details their virtues of love, devotion, and resiliency. She has crafted an engaging tale of romance, rivalry, and the power of forgiveness." *Library Journal* adds, "Warren's characters are well-developed and she knows how to create a first rate contemporary romance…"

Susan is also a nationally acclaimed writing coach, teaching at conferences around the nation, and winner of the 2009 American Christian Fiction Writers Mentor of the Year award. She loves to help people launch their writing careers. She is the founder of www.MyBookTherapy.com and www.learnhow-towriteanovel.com, a writing website that helps authors get published and stay published. She is also the author of the popular writing method *The Story Equation.*

Find excerpts, reviews, and a printable list of her novels at www.susanmaywarren.com and connect with her on social media.

facebook.com/susanmaywarrenfiction

instagram.com/susanmaywarren

x.com/susanmaywarren

bookbub.com/authors/susan-may-warren

goodreads.com/susanmaywarren

amazon.com/Susan-May-Warren

CONNECT WITH SUNRISE

Thank you again for reading *Flashpoint*. We hope you enjoyed the story. If you did, would you be willing to do us a favor and leave a review? It doesn't have to be long—just a few words to help other readers know what they're getting. (But no spoilers! We don't want to wreck the fun!) Thank you again for reading!

We'd love to hear from you—not only about this story, but about any characters or stories you'd like to read in the future. Contact us at www.sunrisepublishing.com/contact.

We also have a monthly update that contains sneak peeks, reviews, upcoming releases, and fun stuff for our reader friends. Sign up at www.sunrisepublishing.com or scan our QR code.

MORE EPIC ROMANTIC ADVENTURE

CHASING FIRE: MONTANA

Flashpoint by Susan May Warren

Flashover by Megan Besing

Flashback by Michelle Sass Aleckson

Firestorm by Lisa Phillips

Fireline by Kate Angelo

Fireproof by Susan May Warren

MONTANA FIRE BY SUSAN MAY WARREN

Where There's Smoke (Summer of Fire)

Playing with Fire (Summer of Fire)

Burnin' For You (Summer of Fire)

Oh, The Weather Outside is Frightful (Christmas novella)

I'll be There (Montana Fire/Deep Haven crossover)

Light My Fire (Summer of the Burning Sky)

The Heat is On (Summer of the Burning Sky)

Some Like it Hot (Summer of the Burning Sky)

You Don't Have to Be a Star (spin-off)

LAST CHANCE FIRE AND RESCUE BY LISA PHILLIPS

Expired Return

Expired Hope (with Megan Besing)

Expired Promise (with Emilie Haney)

Expired Vows (with Laura Conaway)

LAST CHANCE COUNTY BY LISA PHILLIPS

Expired Refuge

Expired Secrets

Expired Cache

Expired Hero

Expired Game

Expired Plot

Expired Getaway

Expired Betrayal

Expired Flight

Expired End

Made in the USA
Coppell, TX
26 May 2024

32789699R00125